runny eggs

Alison Drury

Christine Hogg

Susan O'Neal

ISBN 9-781446717622

This book is dedicated to all the hotels and cafes that allow
writing friends to commandeer a quiet area
and remain there for much of the day.

Special thanks go to those kitchen staff who actually know
how to cook an egg.

Contents

RAW

Runny Eggs 1

Death's Head Hawkmoth 7

I Would Have Preferred 9

Bailey 16

Coping With Change 18

Sorry 25

His Name Was Ethan 27

Her Most Precious Possession 33

PICKLED

Let's Start Over 43

Just Visiting 54

The Letter 58

Interim Report 64

Terminal 66

Motivation 72

A Vase and the Marigolds 79

I am Ventor 85

Freedom Day 90

Modnitsy 98

Ditched 103

HARD BOILED

An Unhappy Accident 107

Investigator Required 110

Jewels 115

The Rules of the Game 120

Blood Ties 125

The Method 142

Kevin's Insurance Policy 146

You Should Have Said 151

Trapped 157

SCRAMBLED

The Poacher 163

Why is a Raven Like a Writing Desk? 168

A Day Trip to Tangier 174

Currant Tensions 185

Good Things Come To Those Who Wait 189

Raw

The fragility of life and emotion

Runny Eggs

Susan O'Neal

'Let's meet at the doughnut stand on Waterloo Station,' I'd said.

We hadn't been up to London for months and months, what with the pandemic and everyone being nervous about Going Out. The Government said they were working hard behind the scenes to make everything better and we should be patient. They had a plan. Their slogan was 'Fortitude'. But after a while, we simply wanted to see each other face to face. We decided to celebrate our joint birthdays in style.

When I got there, I saw things had changed since lockdown. The stalls of doughnuts, tourist souvenirs and hanging packets of sweets had been swept away. There were no magazine stands or any of the overflowing rubbish bins I remembered, with odd scraps of paper blowing along the walkways like urban tumbleweed. Instead the spotless concourse was edged with long panels of sterile plate glass, topped with handrails of shiny metal tubing. Hastily, I sent a text to the other two: I've changed location - I'm near the main stairs now.

While I waited, I watched the ant-like trails of bodies criss-crossing the space in every direction, everyone anonymous behind face masks. A few folk fingered the new accessories self-consciously but most seemed resigned to following the rules. Nearly everyone had a smartphone, either clamped to their ears or held in front, fingers texting, not watching where they were going. I marvelled there were no collisions. Time and again a little chassé step to the side avoided what had seemed an inevitable crash - what sixth sense was in play here?

When my friends arrived, Celia had on a futuristic face covering like a space helmet and Angela was sporting a multicoloured flowery mask, embroidered with trembling butterflies. My own boring blue pleated number hid my grin. We exchanged air kisses and set off across the raised walkway towards the Festival Hall, discussing where to have brunch before shopping for our fortieth birthday presents.

'What about the café on the upper deck? I had a delicious meal there last year,' I suggested.

The other two were happy with that and within a very few moments we were sitting in a cosy booth. Notices everywhere warned we could only remove our face coverings to eat. We hastily reached for the menus. Posh versions of buttery egg on toast were on offer, with bacon and even avocado. Our choices made, it proved impossible to attract a waiter's eye. This should have warned us. The place wasn't busy. Apart from us, there was one other customer busy on his phone with an empty cup in front of him. Two waiters enjoyed a chat with their backs to us.

Time was short and we were hungry so Celia went over to the counter to give our order.

Eventually a pot of tea and two coffees arrived and then some cutlery, wrapped in paper napkins. So far, so good. Ish. We relinquished the masks and sipped our drinks.

When the plates arrived, ten minutes later, they felt cold. Celia's egg wasn't properly cooked, the white beneath a thin skin emerging like a glutinous opalescent sneeze. She wrinkled her nose with distaste.

Angela and I explored our eggs gingerly.

'Mine's okay, just not very warm,' said Angela bravely.

Mine was slightly better cooked but stone cold.

'I can't eat that.' Celia poked at the eggs.

'Are you going to send them back?'

Celia was, and finally got a waitress's attention by dint of leaning outwards from the booth and waving wildly. The girl took the plate away, warning it would be seven minutes before a replacement would be delivered. A curiously precise prediction, we thought.

Meantime, Angela and I decided our meals were really not up to scratch, cold and not enjoyable, so when Celia's eggs arrived, we expressed our disappointment, with reasons, and our plates were borne away without a word.

While we waited, Celia discovered the replacement eggs were equally inedible and cold. She pushed the plate aside with a moue of distaste.

When our second set of food was brought, we had to ask for cutlery with which to eat it. When that arrived, we discovered the eggs were, if anything, worse than the first lot. Cold and uncooked.

'I'm going to complain.' I looped my mask around my ears and strode up to the bar to ask for the manager. The waitress explained there wasn't a manager on duty, but could she help.

So I told her. Of our disappointment, the runny cold eggs, the indifferent service.

'I'm so sorry,' she said, 'I'll go and talk to the kitchen.'

'We don't think we should pay for what we've been served.' I was revving up to do battle but it wasn't necessary.

'Of course,' she soothed and set off to have her conversation. She came back almost immediately.

'I can only apologise. We seem to be having a problem,' she said, which didn't feel like an explanation of what had gone wrong. We left, muttering darkly of our intention never to darken their doors again.

'How can you mess up eggs on toast?' said Celia. 'You'd have thought it was one of the first things anyone learned to cook.'

'I think it was deliberate,' I said.

The other two turned to me, Celia raising an interrogative eyebrow.

'Didn't you think it was odd, the whole place so empty at Saturday lunchtime? There's plenty of people everywhere along the riverside, but all the cafés we've passed are practically deserted. There was only that one man, and us, when we sat down. I think the terrible service was done on purpose to keep people out.'

'I can't imagine where you get your ideas,' said Angela. 'Explain.'

By now we were causing a bit of a blockage on the walkway, and people were muttering about social distancing, so we moved to a vacant bench and sat down.

'The whole place felt weird. The booths were the same as I remember, but the atmosphere was off.'

'What on earth are you talking about?' Celia wasn't having any of this. 'You've been reading too much science fiction.'

'No seriously, think about it for a moment. When we got to the station, it felt different didn't it? Altered somehow. Didn't you notice?'

'Well I saw the doughnut stand had gone- ' Celia began.

'Exactly. And the souvenir places and the sweets. In fact anything that would tempt a tourist or an impulse buyer.'

'And all the cafés we passed seemed bland and unwelcoming. As well as empty.'

'Yes, I saw that. There used to be a whole range of different sorts- '

'Exactly. I think the New Order is starting.'

Angela was horrified. 'It can't be. They said it wouldn't, not until everyone agreed.'

'Perhaps it's taking too long to get everyone on side. Maybe the government has moved things along.'

'They can't do that, can they? What about the Consultation?'

'Look around you. What do you think?'

We looked. We'd already seen the empty cafés, but now we registered other things.

'The entrances to the underground were closed,' Angela began. 'I thought it was for maintenance but maybe- '

'Everywhere is the same silvery grey, almost as if the colour of everything has leached away.'

'And there's something else,' I said. 'Where are all the old people?'

'Never mind about old people,' said Celia, 'I haven't seen anyone older than us, have you?'

We stared at each other. I shivered.

'What do you think 'Fortitude' means?'

Death's Head Hawkmoth

Alison Drury

At sixteen our melancholic creativity made our teachers uneasy. The stencilled moths with their death's-head skulls stared, empty-eyed, from our satchel flaps and exercise books. We lamented the loss of something unknown but grieved for it anyway, in our black lace and velvet.

The whistle blew. We moved like sloths. Physical education lessons were the antithesis of our inertia. Anything more strenuous than running from the school bus to avoid the rain led to streaky eyeliner and raised purple blotchy skin. Primary yellow vests highlighted the dark circles under our eyes, and the clammy Aertex provoked chafing from the piercings on our peely-wally skin.

Last out of the changing room, we dragged our feet to the back of the start line. We cut our own route for the cross-country runs and shared a smoke behind the science block, before ambling in last with nothing more than nicotine-stained fingers and peppermint breath. No exertion, no sweat, no shower. First out of the changing room. Doddle.

At eighteen we drifted into art-school heaven and all was hunky-dory, David Bowie, and bohemian living. Long nights talking Radcliffe and Poe, reading Dickinson and listening to Joy Division. Neo-expressionists, searching for the light in the darkness with dour acrylics and monochromatic linocuts.

Then Rosie died. What the fuck?!

An aneurysm they said. A hyper explosion of red that spattered me with anger and guilt and sadness. I stopped smoking, gave up caffeine, became a kaleidoscopic veggie pescatarian. I ran and ran and cried and cried. I ran for Rosie. I ran for charity. I ran some more, and the caged raven gradually shapeshifted into an enlightened canary.

Now I run and run. I can't stop. It's an addiction. My own private narcotic called 'Rosie' explodes in my brain; helps me forget. Helps me remember. Makes me feel so good. Should I thank Rosie for dying? That sounds absurd but what would have become of us if she hadn't? Would we be junkies: dead anyway? Would we have become respectable but bored: dead anyway? I run, and my Rosies are released; she vitalises me.

I Would Have Preferred

Christine Hogg

'Carly? Did you say something?' Graham called to me from the hallway.

'Sorry, no, I was just... '

'Just what?' His eager face appeared around the doorframe, followed by his tall, lanky body – draped as always in a huge baggy t-shirt.

'Nothing. Doesn't matter.'

'You can talk to me about nothing - or anything,' he said, smiling his wide caring smile.

I carried on putting the groceries away. I stood for a while, studying the lettuce. A big Iceberg variety, which was fine. I would have preferred Little Gem, the ones with small leaves... kind of soft, but textured, crinkly... nice taste, bitter but almost buttery. Crinkly bitterly buttery.

'What?' Graham loomed over me, making me jump. I wish he wouldn't do that.

'Nothing,' I said. 'I didn't say anything.'

I rotated the lettuce in my hands, looking at the wide, watery, nothing-tasting leaves. As I turned it around, the price sticker came into view. 50% off. So that explained it. The thing was nearly the size of a football. I wondered what would happen if I kicked it through the window.

'Are you okay?' he asked. 'Are... are we okay?'

'Of course.' I turned to put the lettuce in the fridge.

I felt his big hands on my waist and he pulled me in towards him.

'Isn't this amazing?' he said. 'Our own place. Just us.' He bent to kiss my neck. I resisted the urge to brush him away. I pictured a limp salad, technically food, perfectly adequate, but still... Maybe there was something more exciting in the bag?

I went to get the rest of the groceries. 'Just need to get these in the fridge.'

'What's the rush?' He smiled. His wide brown eyes crinkling at the sides.

'They'll get warm.'

He laughed and glanced at the thermometer. Just a little eye-movement, not even shifting his head. Just enough to remind me that it was still early spring and chilly. I tried not to shiver. We hadn't sorted out the heating yet. We planned to fix it later in the year, before winter.

I reached into a shopping bag and picked out a pack of tomatoes. Beef tomatoes. Big and squashy, overripe and the colour fading. Not the sweet little cherry ones that burst with flavour as you bite into them. Not the small scarlet capsules of tangy deliciousness, firm and colourful alongside grapes and olives in a salad. Perfect with crinkly Little Gem lettuce leaves and cubes of crumbly Cheshire cheese and a small hunk of freshly baked wholemeal bread

– still warm from the oven, oozing with gently melting butter.

No. These were hulking great tomatoes that you have to slice with a carving knife so the seeds go everywhere and leave liquid all over the bread board because he hasn't bought a proper chopping board yet, like he promised. These were probably force-raised in some giant factory farm, drenched in chemicals until they swelled to monster proportions. Enormous, tasteless, unattractive.

'What?' he said, towering over me.

I shook my head. Why was he always ... here.

He looked down at me, waiting.

'Sorry, I was just thinking about dinner. I'm pretty hungry.'

Iceberg lettuce, and beef tomatoes. Good for nothing but laying on top of a processed cheese slice, drooping over an economy burger. Better still with cheap white bread rolls, the big fat type that stick to the roof of your mouth, making a claggy ball that you chew and chew but just can't swallow.

I put my hand back into the bag and pulled out a large pack of jumbo white bread rolls.

'Special offer,' Graham said, proudly. 'I got some burgers too. Twelve for one pound ninety-nine.'

Of course he did. I took a deep breath and held onto the counter.

'I would have preferred...' I started, but his brow furrowed, his eager smile beginning to falter.

'What darling? Talk to me.' He put his arms around me again, nuzzling into my neck. I let my shoulders relax against him, clenching my jaw and pressing my lips together. It was only bread and tomatoes.

* * *

I watched my friend Marie's face on the screen. Her tongue was sticking out as she concentrated, pressing buttons. I waited until she found the right one.

'There you are,' she grinned. 'Are you alone?'

'Yes. He's popped over to his mum's.'

'Fabulous,' she said. 'Give me all the gossip. You've been living together... what... two weeks? How's it going.'

'Oh it's all fine. How have you been?'

'Fine?' she asked. 'Come on, tell me all about it.'

I laughed. I should have known she wouldn't let me get away with that.

'It's great. He's doing all the shopping and cooking – he likes that. While I do the cleaning, so, it's all fair, I guess, domestically.'

'But?' she asked.

'Nothing. I mean seriously, I have nothing to complain about.'

'But?'

'He just keeps... well... he buys cheap things.'

'What sort of things?'

'Tomatoes for one.'

'Tomatoes?'

'Beef tomatoes, and iceberg lettuce. Jumbo white rolls. Anything that's on special offer. The bigger and more tasteless and boring the better.'

Marie snorted and stared at me from the screen, her eyes wide.

'What?' I asked.

'Well he's very tall so I imagine he needs to eat a lot – and he's being careful with money – that's a good thing, isn't it?'

'Yes, of course, but–'

'But what? Iceberg lettuce can't be a problem. What's really going on?'

'That's it... that's really it.'

'He's not beating you? Locking you in the house? Making you sleep in the basement.'

'No, he's being really lovely. It's just the food. It's... well... unexciting.'

'What were you expecting? Caviar and oysters?'

'I... I pictured us having romantic dinners, lovely salads, nothing too fancy, just... nice things... not everything being... dull.'

'But iceberg lettuce makes a lovely salad... my family never complain... and since when have you cared about food anyway?'

I tried not to roll my eyes. I knew where this was going.

'Remember at university?'

I resisted the urge to shut down the zoom call. 'Alright, we both know I lived off pasta and pot noodles, but I had a student loan.'

'And now you have a mortgage and a baby on the way.'

I nodded. Not trusting myself to speak. She was much better at all this domestic stuff than me. I pulled myself together, pasted a big smile on my face.

'It's all just taking a bit of getting used to. I've always made my own decisions... bought what I fancied.'

'Why don't you do the shopping?'

I laughed. 'Then I'd have to cook... and I'm not quite ready to let him find out that pot noodle is the limit of my culinary skills.'

* * *

As the summer progressed, I became more and more uncomfortable. Both from the heat and the increasingly visible reality of my pregnancy. I was going to be a mother and I was petrified... trapped. All my freedom to choose alternatives was gone. I had to provide a stable home for a little person. I couldn't breathe.

Some days were better than others. There were small windows when I felt like myself again.

One evening in August, when I was six months pregnant, I sat down for dinner at a table that had been decked out with candles and a white table-cloth. I felt like crying. To be fair most things at that point made me feel like crying, but this was just so lovely, what I'd been longing for. I almost couldn't bear it. It was the little things that most affected me, pleasant touches to make life a bit less mundane, to make me feel a bit more special.

He smiled as he brought the plates from the kitchen and presented them with a flourish, his beautiful blue eyes crinkling as they gazed into mine.

Fillet of sea bass with fennel, a glossy white sauce and little sprigs of parsley. I'd argued with Graham about this just the week before. So stupid, fighting over fish, but he just couldn't seem to understand that a bumper pack of boil-in-the bag cod in butter sauce wasn't a treat... it wasn't special, especially served with huge dollops of microwaved mashed potatoes.

This was more like it.

He strolled back to the kitchen and I admired his confident walk. His tanned, firm chest under a tight-fitting shirt. He came back with a large white bowl, little salad leaves and a rainbow of cherry tomatoes, black and green olives, sweet pimento peppers, baby spring onions, even grapes.

'I'm not entirely convinced this goes with fish,' he grinned. 'But I tried to include things that you like.'

That was it, I burst into tears. It felt so wonderful to be listened to, to be heard.

After we finished eating we held hands for a long time.

'Scary times ahead,' he said, and reached out to stroke my belly. 'Things will never be the same again.'

I sighed and tried to hold back the tears.

He looked at his watch and groaned.

'You'd better be getting back to Graham. He'll be wondering where you are.'

Bailey

Alison Hogg

The gnarled oak door was latched; a barricade against the late winter chill. Inside, the stone cowshed was snug and warm, with the sweet aroma of freshly laid straw. The only sounds were Gertie's occasional snort and the rustle as she circled impatiently, waiting to calf. Her movements threw up rotating silver motes from the high window as Bailey sat with her through the night. She was his last remaining milker, but, unfortunately, this was to be his first step into retirement; in the morning the vet was called. It had been too much of a struggle for poor Gertie.

Bailey had worked the farm all his life and had never married; always said the farm kept him in his place and gave him back everything he ever wanted. He lived in the farmhouse with his sister, who was known by everyone as Grandma.

Gradually, over the next few years, the farm was wound up, Grandma passed away, and the younger members of the family decided to convert the cowshed into a little cottage where Bailey could enjoy his final years. However, the constant delays with planning permission and the Bat Conservation Trust, together with finding a sympathetic builder, exacerbated his gout. He grumbled from his wheelchair and pointed with his pitchfork as the builders tore down the pigsties, levelled the bank and dug trenches for the drains. Slowly, it came together; the wee potting shed around the side was new, as was the veranda across the back with views to the Downs. But the Kent peg tiles and little window in the eaves remained, and the big oak door frame now had a triple glazed insert revealing the ever-changing landscape.

Unfortunately, Bailey never saw inside his new home - but he did visit. Snug in his casket, surrounded by the cloying perfume of roses and arum lilies, he was set in front of the big picture window for forty-five minutes before the procession.

Coping With Change

Susan O'Neal

The seventh day in my new flat, I found a worm in the fridge. It was flat, black and dead. I quite like interesting animals, but not this one - it looked remarkably like a leech. Where had that come from? I live in the centre of a city where supermarket veggies are sold sealed in sterile plastic bags. Which is not great for the environment of course, but at least people know what they're getting and someone else has already trimmed and washed the stuff (or possibly not!) Gingerly I double-bagged the corpse and put it in the freezer. Eric might fancy it later.

* * *

By the time I had tipped everything out of the fridge and used quantities of bleach to disinfect it thoroughly, I had lost nearly an hour and was running late for my meeting with Stephanie. And not quite as fragrant as I might have been. I'd built up quite a sweat, with all that scrubbing, and the all-pervasive smell of Domestos does cling, rather. I had no time to shower or even change, so I peeled off the yellow rubber gloves, gave myself a generous swoosh of Coty's *L'Aimant* and sallied forth into the High Street, hoping for the best.

* * *

'So, Debbie - tell me what you hope to get out of this session?'

This was her classic counsellor opening gambit, with her head tilted to one side, a bright smile fixed on her perfectly made-up face.

I mumbled something about finding myself, looking for the new me, all the sort of guff I had come to understand she would be expecting, and off we went on our usual routine. She probed with empathy, and I deflected as neutrally as I could, while trying to remain as convincing as possible. We volleyed our conversational ball back and forth for half an hour or so before Stephanie sat back, drawing her notes towards her. She spent a moment or two pretending to review the information, leafing between the little pile of pages she had amassed during the previous two sessions.

Although irritating, I admired her performance and waited, as patiently as I could, for her summary. I had worked quite hard not to give much away, while laying a crumb trail for her to discover. Attending these therapy sessions was mandatory but that didn't mean I had to like them or believe they were going to do me any good. I just wanted the damn anti-depressants. My old fashioned family doctor wouldn't dish them out until I'd been to three counselling sessions. This was the last one.

'So, Debbie -' (this was getting old, she always started her questions like that) 'how do you think you are getting on?'

'Aren't you supposed to be telling me that?' It was difficult to keep the asperity from my voice. I had to remember you catch more flies with honey than vinegar. Careful Debbie, be very careful.

'Well, yes, but I'd like to hear your opinion first.'

I wasn't about to tell her that coming here hadn't made a jot of difference.

'Now that I've actually left home and moved into my new flat, I do feel a little bit calmer, I guess...' I began hesitantly. I was supposed to be anxious, she needed to see that. 'But I still worry a lot.'

'So, Debbie - what's worrying you, at this very moment?'

Predictable. More head tilting and her pen was poised to capture my particular misgivings.

'I'm worrying about how I'm going to cope, on my own, now that our sessions are coming to an end.'

'Yes, I can see how that could be an issue,' admitted Stephanie.

The funding only covered three meetings. I had already mentioned I couldn't afford a private course of consultations.

'Have you thought of getting a cat? For company,' she suggested brightly.

'Pets are not allowed in the flats,' I said.

'Or a budgie?' she asked, clearly not listening properly.

'I hate anything caged up - things with wings should be allowed to fly.'

She ruffled through the notes, but I think we both knew she had run out of options. She looked up and there was a long pause while she gazed intently into my face. I forced myself to look away, down at my clasped hands. I tried a little dispirited sigh. I was just wondering whether I could squeeze out a tear when Stephanie made up her mind.

'I think I'll have to confirm to Doctor Morgan that a course of anti-depressants would be appropriate. A short course,' she added quickly, 'just to get you back on track, so to speak.'

At last. About time too. I nodded solemnly.

She made a note on her pad and drew a rather obvious line underneath it. She turned back her cuff to check her watch. Not subtle. I got the point. I had things to do, too.

'Thank you for your help Stephanie,' I said politely as I retrieved my bag and stood up.

'Look after yourself,' she said as she moved across the room to open the door for me.

Yeah, well, I knew how to do that, alright. I was out of her pale green consulting room and down the street before she had a chance to say anything else. I guessed it would be a week or so until her notes would be typed up and sent to my doctor with the recommendations. That would just about give me time to get everything else ready.

* * *

Smuggling Eric into my new flat on the third floor was going to be tricky. It's not easy to disguise an eight foot purple dragon and Eric was prone to snorting flames when he got anxious. When I explained to him that he had to move location, he had waggled his head apprehensively and puffed a little stream of warm vapour from his left nostril.

He was jammed into the U-Store container I'd been renting for the last month, with barely enough room to turn round now, let alone stretch out or flex his wings. I hadn't realised he would grow quite so quickly and there was no denying the diet suited him. Fortunately there was no shortage of old car tyres and road kill round about where I live, so he was cheap to keep, even if his provisions were heavy to deliver. I had decided if I could just manage Eric's flame throwing tendencies, the rest would be fairly straightforward. Which is where the anti-depressants came in. I thought if they worked for people, they might help calm a dragon sufficiently that we could slip quietly up six flights of stairs into the flat, under cover of darkness. Clearly I'd need quite a large quantity, given the size of him. With any luck, I'd have a couple of months' supply soon and if Eric was reluctant to take them, I thought I could try disguising the pills in the worm. I'd read somewhere that people who kept hawks fed them on day old chicks and I had space in the freezer for a few, if I could get hold of some. If all else failed, I was pretty sure the pet shop sold small rodents, no questions asked.

Another challenge would be covering the noise once he was installed. Eric sleeps a good percentage of the day but at night time, he needs to get out and about. Just flexing his leather-like wings ready to leave makes quite a racket and the first flew flaps of his muscular shoulders as he launches himself into the air produces a series of slapping noises that echo like gunshots in the night air. I thought some classical jazz played exuberantly might work. I had downloaded a number of tracks and been playing them increasingly loudly for the last week. None of the people in the flats had said anything so far, so hopefully I'd got that covered. I had managed to avoid the neighbours since I'd moved in, even dodging the woman who had come up four separate times and rung my bell - I really didn't want to be doing with strangers, now I had Eric.

* * *

It had started, as these things often do, by accident. I have always liked curiosities and on a day trip to Caernarvon Castle in the summer I had picked up an interesting shaped stone in the grounds and brought it home. I had put it on my bedroom window ledge, intending to use it for the base of an air-plant display, to give to Mum. I suppose the warmth of the sun, concentrated though the window, had delivered the optimum level of heat and within a week, a crack had appeared. The next day an adorable little leathery lizard had emerged to sun itself in the August warmth.

The following months had been a joy, helping him learn to fly, once his wings were fully developed. I stopped going out, absorbed with my new pet. I got away with the first accident, I told Mum I'd left a cigarette burning. She seemed to have forgotten I gave up smoking a year ago - she's not that interested in my life, not really. For all our sakes, I had quietly rented the storage unit, smuggled Eric out and started looking for a top floor flat with big windows.

    And now, here I am in my new place, with another dilemma - the smoke detector in the ceiling is wired into the mains.

Sorry

Christine Hogg

I jump when I see them. Little bulging eyes stare as light floods the driveway, triggered by the sensor. Tiny shadows leap into hedges and borders. Leaves rustle as they flee.

'I'm sorry,' I say.

It isn't enough.

The light cuts out. I must see if we can extend the timer, the route from the garage to the front door is pitch black by the time I get home.

A soft weight lands on my shoe. I freeze. After a moment I lean back towards the sensor and wave. Nothing happens. I flap my arms frantically, feet rooted to the spot like one of those air-filled tubes that dance outside garages. The night stays dark.

I slowly start to rotate my foot, hoping the little creature will hop off. I feel it shift. The soft body starts to crawl over my stocking. I shudder and kick out, waving my foot in a demented devil's hokeycokey; losing my shoe.

Everything alright?' My neighbour's voice comes from the other side of the fence.

'Frogs,' I say, hopping towards the edge of the building, finally triggering the light.

'Toads,' he corrects me. 'Used to live in your pond, before you filled it in.

I could feel his disapproving glare through the fence.

'I told you they'd be back,' he continued. 'Every year. Instinct. Looking for their home.'

'Yes,' I say. Biting my tongue to stop another 'sorry' escaping. The pond had stunk, and we wanted the space for a patio.

I hear him muttering as he walks away.

'Bloody town folk.'

His Name Was Ethan

Alison Drury

Piper curled up in the worn wicker chair in the summer house at the bottom of the garden. Wrapped in an old blanket she watched a jet silently paint a white trail across the clear sky. Within moments, the garden had melted away and morphed into her familiar fantasy world.

[His name was Ethan. A dark obelisk in his black boots, skinny black jeans and black leather bike jacket which stretched taut across his broad shoulders. His hair, so black it had a bluish lustre, framed a square face with strong jaw and navy-blue eyes with thick black lashes. As he passed, he turned to stare and his eyes narrowed in puzzlement. And then he was gone, riding his board along the broad promenade. She'd lost count how many times this had happened.

She sat on the bench facing out to sea and watched the tide turning, frothing between the polished pebbles and dragging the bladderwrack as it receded. The sun balanced on the horizon, bleeding orange light into the water as day capsized into night.

Maybe her half smile had triggered the puzzled look he gave her. That was promising; tomorrow she would say something.]

Do you have beautiful dreams? Do you wish they were real and that you could pick up where you left off from the night before? Piper's dreams were like that. Vivid and cinematic - so real, she didn't even have to be asleep. She wrote the script and created her own world.

[The pheasant grass waved in the wind like parachute silk, fanning the scent of catmint and lavender whirling in its wake. She sat on the sea wall, tracking the gulls which were keowing and circling on the thermals under the cliffs; the sun picking out the amber inclusions in her green eyes. She heard a rumble and glanced towards the sound. This time he stopped in front of her and tapped the end of his board with his toe and caught it as it flipped into the air.

Piper held her breath, surprised even at her own inventiveness. She watched as he planted a large black boot on the wall beside her and leaned forward to gently pull on a spiral of her coppery hair. So close, she could taste the cocktail of leather and lavender on her tongue.

'Hi,' his voice was deep and smooth like luxury ice cream.

She licked her lips, 'Hello.'

'I'm Ethan.'

'I know,' she said. 'I'm Piper.'

And so it began, again.]

* * *

She remembered how she had screamed every day when her mother left her at the classroom door. After a few weeks of not 'growing out of it', the teachers had despaired. 'Attention seeker' they called her. Disruptive students were sent to sit on their own - perfect. She would disappear into a parallel universe where she invented friends and had imaginary adventures.

Ethan had been there from the beginning; her best friend, her playmate. She had reinvented him several times now and this was her new Ethan.

[They met regularly at the beach now and their crazy brains shared everything. This was the best Ethan so far. She never wanted to wake up. The music in her headphones became their soundtrack and drove the narrative. He became vivid and real with a new backstory; an only child of busy parents he often felt alone and forgotten, a burden, an afterthought. She decided that the next time they met she would invite him home.]

She was sent for tests. The doctors prodded and poked, she had scans and they wrote statements. It could be anxiety, or narcolepsy, or some form of autism. They could offer no definitive diagnosis. They prescribed pills, but little did they know she'd stashed the pills in an old tin under the bed. She loved her world and fought to keep it.

It had been decided she should try psychodynamic therapy. Talking about her feelings and dreams might help her, and them, understand. Today was her fifth appointment. Again, the waiting room had been empty; nobody had gone in or come out while she had been there. Maybe they staggered the patients to avoid curiosity and potentially destructive self-judgment.

'Go in Piper, Dr Ericsson will see you now,' the receptionist peered over her spectacles and gestured with her head.

Piper tucked her headphones into her pocket and walked into the consulting room.

The doctor put down her pen and directed her to the armchair, 'How are you today?'

Piper sat down but didn't look up, 'I'm fine.'

Dr Ericsson came around and leaned on the front of her desk. 'I've been reviewing our sessions and there's something I'd like to try if you feel up to it?'

Piper shrugged, 'Okay.'

'I'd like you to meet someone - another patient with similar symptoms to you. Would you be willing to consider it? I think it might help both of you if you could share your experiences.'

[She never discussed the therapy sessions with Ethan. That was another life. Summer came and went and by late September he had finally come to her house. Huddled on the summer house veranda, they watched a meteor shower crashing through the atmosphere. The old blanket sparkled with evening dew, but she was cosy, tucked under Ethan's arm, her cheek warm against his chest, and they counted the falling stars. She fell with them, into the rhythm of their breathing until their heartbeats became pink noise.]

Piper arrived first. She sat and waited nervously. She had never doubted she was a little strange – but others seemed more bothered about it than her. However, Dr Ericsson's comments had piqued her interest. Were there others out there like her? Google had thrown up a term called 'maladaptive daydreaming' with thousands of online views. Perhaps she wasn't so strange after all.

['Ethan? Ethan!' She was agitated, it had been like wading through marshmallow but finally, she had made it to the beach. It was deserted. Debris was strewn everywhere, brought in on the storm which had been raging for days. Even the seagulls had taken flight inland. The bench, set back in the chalk of the undercliff, offered a respite from the whirling wind. Tufts of marram grass, torn from the sand dunes way down on the foreshore, tumbled and bounced over the pebbles at this end of the beach and became wrapped around her legs. Her dream, like Wagoner's Tumbleweed, yawed away as soon as it was let go.

'No! Stop, stop.' Frantically, she tried to direct her vision, to conjure up calm - and Ethan. She clung to the bench as the wind cackled and whipped her hair like rusty nails stinging her eyes.

'Come back!' But her screech was snatched by the wind. The cloying wet air condensed and sucked any remaining colour to grey. Everything went dark.]

* * *

He stood across the road opposite the clinic, like he had every time, and waited until the very last minute before going in. As far as he was concerned it was just a tick-box exercise and would keep his parents off his back. His life was peachy, he made sure of it. He'd found the perfect girl and no amount of therapy or coercing would sway him to re-join a world where he was awkward and had no prospects. He nodded at the receptionist as she indicated for him to go through and wasn't surprised to see someone already in his seat. The thought of Dr Ericsson's little experiment had been making him anxious for days, to the point he had blocked out everything, including that special place he escaped to.

Entering the consulting room, he took a moment to focus on the mini-mindfulness technique that Dr Ericcson had taught him. 'Focus on what you can see, feel, and touch - ignore the insecurities that only exist inside your head'. Finally, he moved towards the centre of the room just as a mass of copper spirals spun round to reveal the heart-shaped face he knew so well. He was stunned. His eyes skimmed over her casual stonewashed jeans, loafers and wrap-around cardigan but it was the effect of her soft emerald green scarf set against her fiery hair that took his breath away.

'Hello,' her voice was soft and sweet like honey.

He licked his lips, 'Hi.'

'I'm Piper.'

'I know,' he said, twitching the corner of his mouth. 'I'm Ethan.'

And so it began, for real.

Her Most Precious Possession

Susan O'Neal

Without opening her eyes, she knew. At some level of her subconscious she had been counting down the days until today. Michael was there beside her, breathing lightly but regularly and she wouldn't disturb him. Fully awake now, she lay still, trying to quieten the clamorous thoughts crowding into her head and get back to sleep. After what seemed like hours, she gave up and rose slowly and silently, padding down the landing into the bathroom. Returning to their room, Claire lifted her clothes from the chair at the foot of the bed and took them downstairs, to dress while the kettle came to the boil. Hugging her mug of tea to herself as a form of comfort, she stood gazing out onto the garden. It had never looked better. The roses were nodding their perfumed heads in the weed-free borders, the vegetable plot was astonishingly prolific this year and the lawn was a lush velvet carpet. A pair of robins were on the new birdfeeder, darting in and out of the cupped feeder, politely taking turns. Clearly they liked that new buttery stuff, she should order some more.

Claire wondered how long she had. There might be weeks left before the sky fell in. Or days. Would it be any better if she knew exactly? Probably not. She sighed and set down her mug, reaching for the used plates and glasses left on the table the night before. They had drunk a good deal more wine than usual yesterday and abandoned the clearing up in a blurry happy haze. Slotting the dishes carefully into their places in the dishwasher, Claire set the thing off. She couldn't understand why anyone would want to be up to their elbows in greasy water, washing pots by hand these days. Or washing clothes by hand - who did that in the twenty-first century? Those without the means to buy the convenient appliances of course, her inner puritan chided her. Enough of this, she wasn't going to think about money problems this early in the day. But it was too late. She had woken the tiger again.

* * *

Ever since that awful afternoon six months ago, she had known this would happen. Moving over to the mirror and tucking her unruly morning hair behind her ears, she contemplated her reflection. Her earrings sparkled, catching the early morning light. Turning her head this way and that, she admired the effect. She'd always worn solitaire studs, ever since admiring them on one of the senior directors at her first job, all those years ago. She aspired to the lifestyle they represented, the subtle suggestion that successful people could afford such an investment of glamour. Hers had been glass and required constant cleaning to keep the reflection sharp. That was one of the ways you could tell real diamonds from the fakes - they twinkled even when they were grubby. Synthetics quickly grew dull and lifeless. But from a distance, and assuming they had had their weekly attention from the combination of washing-up liquid and the electric toothbrush, hers had always passed muster. 'My husband...' she would murmur with a smile, if anyone asked. She would catch their envious glance which took in Michael's handsome profile, his dark curly hair and the protective arm that nearly always encircled her waist when they were out together. That public demonstration of affection.

* * *

If Claire had been a writer, she could have sprinkled any number of clues for her reader to give a hint about her situation. She could have set the scene where our heroine had finally been given real solitaire diamonds but pawned them without telling her husband, to raise money for something secret. Now, for some reason, she needed the real earrings back but she had no cash to redeem them and she was about to be exposed. Or perhaps, longing desperately for the 'real thing' she might have had the opportunity to 'earn' genuine solitaires, like Diana in Indecent Proposal, only to realise that she was pregnant as a result. Or, in a fit of pique over something her partner had said, she'd splashed out on her credit card to buy the real diamonds she had craved for so long. Now the bill was due and she could neither hide it, nor pay it.

Claire however, was not a writer, but a real woman with a real dilemma that she couldn't think her way out of. She turned from the mirror and set about preparing breakfast, glancing at the clock to see how much time she had before she needed to go upstairs again to wake Michael. He always slept deeply, while she ghosted in and out of dreams, waking at dawn or even before sometimes, lying still, trying not to disturb her husband although heaven knew, in reality it would take something dramatic like an earthquake to wake him before he had slept his usual eight hours.

* * *

When the specialist confirmed the nagging pain in her back was, as she suspected, stage four, she decided she would tell no-one. She had seen enough of how things changed for other people in a similar situation, and the last thing she wanted was pity, or sentimental hopeful mantras from folk who were inevitably thanking their lucky stars it wasn't them with the awful news. She hated fuss and dependency but most of all the curtailment of her liberty. She could imagine the endless stream of hospital appointments and hateful interventions that wouldn't change anything, in the long run. The doctor had said it wouldn't take long, the cancer was aggressive and had invaded most of her skeleton already.

On her way home she had locked herself into a restroom cubicle at the station and lost control, howling like a demented fool. What an idiot. Had it been worth it? It was a release of sorts but she wouldn't do it again. When she emerged to wash her tear-streaked face, the cleaner in her pink overall paused in her mopping.

'You alright lovey?'

Not one to share private matters, Claire tried to brush off the query but couldn't speak.

'Can I help?'

Mutely, Claire shook her head. No-one could help her now.

'Bit of a facer isn't it - news like that.' The cleaner was speaking into the mirror as she wiped the taps. 'A person might give anything to change things.'

Claire stared at the woman's back. 'What do you mean?'

The cleaner turned towards Claire and looked straight at her.

'Well, if you had a chance, you might want to arrange things differently. Seeing as how things are, now, for you.'

The lines of her face shimmered, changed shape, and then snapped back but not before Claire thought she glimpsed a dark shadowy oval with glistening almond eyes. She rubbed her own eyes, all that crying must have screwed her vision. The woman was waiting for her response and, without thinking, Claire blurted out. 'Bad news. Not coping right now. I don't want this.'

'Of course you don't lovey. What *do* you want?'

'Things as they were, just for a bit, just until I get used to the idea.'

'How long is 'a bit' then, lovey? A week, a month, six months?'

Claire was no fool, she knew her cancer wasn't fixable. But six months' respite would be very welcome right now. Six months when she wouldn't have to worry, deal with her own pain, and Michael's too.

'Six months would be a gift.' she whispered.

'Right you are then, six months it shall be,' said the strange woman in pink. 'But there are conditions...'

* * *

She realised, too late, she should have been more careful with whom she made a bargain. The curious woman had promised her six months' of a perfect pain-free life but then she must disappear, having parted with her most valuable possession. That was the deal. No prolonged leave-taking of the family, no long-term caring role for Michael. She would simply vanish from this life and fade away, out of sight. That was the bargain struck that fateful afternoon in the station toilets. The one thing that she hadn't resolved was how to pay for these final months and the due date was today. The earrings she assumed the woman wanted weren't flawless diamonds, but carefully cut glass. She had to pay with her most valuable possession, that was the agreement. How to get diamonds? Michael and she had always pooled their money and she had no separate savings. It was something she had been puzzling over for weeks and she was no nearer solving it.

* * *

Michael appeared in the doorway, frowsy with sleep, rubbing his hands through his tousled hair.

'Everything okay Cookie? I must have slept through the alarm- '

'Sorry, love, I was just coming up to wake you. Toast okay?'

'Mmm,' he murmured, reaching for a glass. 'Got plans for today?'

'Nothing special,' she smiled, filling his glass with orange juice. Just working out how to finance the rest of my life. 'You?'

'Usual. Gotta visit a new client to explain a brief that a child of four could have understood from my letter, but they seem to want plenty of personal time for some reason. Dull.' He reached for the toast and buttered it with one swipe of his knife, then crunched into it with relish. 'Any tea left in the pot?'

She poured him a mugful and he stood with his back to the counter, alternately chewing and sipping until he had finished.

'Do you need me to pick anything up on my way home? After last night, we might need more wine...' He winked with comic lasciviousness and she blushed. It had been a good evening, one of the best and they had both enjoyed themselves.

'No? Okay, I'll get dressed and be off then.' He went out, taking the stairs two at a time as usual. She heard the shower start and returned to her musings. It was the two robins, helping themselves in turn to their breakfast, that sparked the idea. She had two credit cards - if she maxed them both out, she could just afford good diamonds. And it wasn't as though she was going to be here when the credit companies realised she couldn't pay. Ordinarily Claire was scrupulously law-abiding but this was an emergency. She wasn't sure what dire retribution would follow when she didn't pay her debt.

It took her all day to travel to the jewellery quarter and buy the earrings. At home, there was no sign of Michael as she prepared their favourite meal of salmon en croute, but he was sometimes late home, if the clients were pernickety. She tried his phone but it went to voicemail.

At eight she began to worry...

Pickled

An unexpected flavour that lasts long in the memory

Let's Start Over

Susan O'Neal

'Excuse me. Who's in charge here?'

I stopped spreading compost and leant on my rake. Out of the corner of my eye I saw Olive was edging backwards, gathering up the empty fertiliser bags. She's programmed to avoid strangers.

'Nobody mate. It's a collective,' I said. Which wasn't strictly true but I wasn't about to explain.

The visitor huffed a bit and shrugged his hands into his jacket pockets.

'Who can I speak to then?'

By now, Olive had eeled her way round the corner of the house, so I was on my own.

'Guess it'll have to be me. What's up?'

He looked a bit awkward but now he'd started, he hadn't got a lot of choice. He pulled a crumpled note from his pocket and launched into his spiel.

'Well, for a start, the residents in this road are fed up with the rubbish in the front garden-'

I held up my hand.

'Stop right there. What rubbish?'

He gestured around the plastic bins and stacks of car tyres lined up next to the fence.

'The compost bins? They're complaining about the compost bins?'

He shrugged. 'Is that what they are? Most people have proper front gardens-'

'No they don't.' I pointed up the road. 'They've all paved over their front gardens and put their cars on them. The only element of garden they have is a few bowls of stunted chrysanthemums and a bay tree in a pot. See for yourself.'

'That's not the point. At least they aren't an eyesore like this.'

'They will be, when it floods. There's nowhere for the water to run off.'

'You're missing the point. People round here don't appreciate what you're doing to this property. The animals for instance. They're noisy and they smell.'

'That's what animals do. The goats and chickens are busy making manure for the garden, while giving us milk and eggs. It's a great system.'

'It might be, in the country. But not in the middle of a city.'

'What difference does it make, if it's a great system?' I was getting into my stride now. 'People need to eat wherever they are. I don't have to drive to the supermarket for my food. Unlike everyone else down this road.'

I was rather pleased with this, turning his argument on its head. He opened his mouth to say something and then closed it again.

'All the animals are really well looked after,' I went on. 'They're healthy and living their best lives. Not like that poor dog at number fourteen that spends all day on its own, crying and scratching at the front door. I can hear it all the way up here.'

'I know what you mean,' said the bloke. 'I live next door-but-two on the other side. I've tried telling them, but they say they have to go to work and there's no-one to look after the dog.'

I wondered why the residents had chosen this guy to be their spokesperson, given his track record. I smiled encouragingly at him.

'What's your name mate?'

'Simon,' he said. 'Simon Metcalf.'

'I'm Gerry,' I said and shook his hand. 'You lived here long?'

'No, Janice and I moved in a couple of months ago. I joined the Residents' Association to get to know folks and found myself on the committee. They said something needed to be done about the smallholding people...'

'And here you are. Well, anyway. Wanna come through and meet some of our animals? No crying and scratching here. Except the chickens, and they're supposed to do that.' I turned to lead the way round the side of the house. I figured he'd probably follow - if he didn't, I'd be rid of him anyway. He followed.

'Hey gang, look who's here - it's Simon from up the road.'

I patted my pocket. Five heads came up and backs were straightened.

'It's weeding day,' I told him, 'and they'd been hard at it for the last hour, so any excuse to take a little break is welcome, as you can imagine.'

I looked around with satisfaction at the bucolic scene. There were lush rows of seedlings and over-wintered sprouts and cabbages, climbing bean wigwams set ready next to the polytunnels and behind them, the neatly netted fruit beds. Animal shelters stood all along the left-hand side, their gates open into the run. The goats were out, munching away as usual and the chickens were pecking about looking for goodies.

'I didn't know you could keep chickens and goats together,' said Simon. 'That's a lot of goats. I know you mentioned milk, but do you eat them as well?'

Was that a shudder? I wasn't sure.

'Absolutely not - we keep them for their milk and manure.'

'Excellent,' said Simon. 'Can I stroke one?'

I nodded and he moved closer to scratch a hairy back.

'It works OK, so long as the goats can't get at the chicken feed - we keep it in the hoppers in the coop. It's funny that. Chickens can eat goats' food with no ill effects at all, but it doesn't work the other way. If the goats get at it, there's spectacular diarrhoea. Shoots out at the speed of sound, all green and lumpy.'

Simon retreated smartly from the goats and looked a little green himself, so I steered him towards the orchard. The bees were making their usual racket, their humming vibrating through the miniature trees as they worked at pollinating. The hum more or less covered the bass rumble from the generators.

'We'll have a good crop this year, if all that blossom sets,' I said, catching Simon's arm and pulling him hastily back from the beeline between the orchard and the row of skeps.

'Don't block their route. They tend to be tetchy if you get in their way. Let me introduce you to the weeding crew. That's Brian in the red jumper, Petey in the stripes, Joe's the one in the straw hat, Olive's in dungarees and that's Cynthia.'

They all smiled and waved at us. Cynthia is a tall curvy woman with spectacular long blonde hair. I'm rather proud of Cynthia. She always attracts a lot of attention and I could tell Simon wasn't immune. I saw him staring. I touched the Botpro in my pocket and had Cynthia wink at him, which made him flush and look away quickly, so he probably didn't spot her metal legs. The crew all bent to their weeding again.

'Do you all live here then? In this house?'

'We do. Now, what else you got on that list then?' I indicated his paper. He looked at it as though he'd never seen it before.

'Um, well, there's the stuff in the front garden-'

'I've explained that, it's where we keep the compost. What else?'

He ran his eye down what looked like a fairly long list of bullet points. He hesitated.

'Actually - it's all nonsense.' He screwed up the paper and pushed it into his pocket. 'I think they might be moaning just because what you're doing is a bit different.'

'I think you're probably right.'

'No hard feelings?'

'None whatsoever. Come back any time. Bring Janice. The more the merrier, always lots to do here. Mucking out and suchlike.'

'Thanks. I will.' I watched him walk slowly back up the pathway, looking around as he went. He gave the goats a wide berth. With a wave, he rounded the corner of the house and was gone. There, I thought, goes an amiable community-minded individual with unusually well-developed common sense. I didn't think he'd be back any time soon.

'OK you lot, he's gone.'

Everyone shambled over to the orchard and sorted themselves into sitting positions under the trees. Cynthia managed well with her chrome pins, but the others were using different means of locomotion. Olive's dungarees hid the wheels very successfully but Joe's single limb was a bit obvious, if you really looked. I keep telling him he would look better as a female with a long skirt, but he's a bit huffy about changing, now he's got used to the padded trousers. Brian and Petey have to stay together, as they share the three legs between them, but they pass muster at a casual glance.

I know the humanoids aren't perfect and when I get a minute I'll have a go at sorting out the lower limb situation. They function well enough for now, to keep the smallholding going, especially when I'm away.

* * *

If there were more than three of us safeguarding this planet, it would be a much more manageable workload. If we could just persuade these ridiculous humans to work together, our job would be a whole lot easier. We think we're winning the battle but the whole process is painfully slow.

I was telling Joel, just last century. 'That's it - we've cracked the world war thing. They won't be doing that again in a hurry.'

He gave me a long look and shook his head.

'Have you learned nothing? They have very short memories.'

And of course, he was right.

We're never entirely sure when the next crisis is going to hit as there are so many variables. But with our early warning system, we can tweak some of the elements. It's not infallible - when the virus unexpectedly got out, we had to play catch up, but that's one of the exceptions. Over the millennia we've headed off meteors, sorted out the dinosaur threat and largely evened out the surface temperature changes, although it's tricky to stay on top of that one, what with the population's interference. They don't help themselves, they really don't.

At least the generators are ready. We're going to need them when the oil runs out. There are two important things to know about generators - they're almost always inconveniently noisy and they're expensive to run - especially with the way fuel prices are skyrocketing. I've finessed old propane units to work almost silently which should be useful. The population will eventually work out how to do that, if we drop enough clues, but I'm most proud of the new power source. I hadn't been entirely honest with Simon about preventing goats eating chicken pellets - that green explosive goo makes the most valuable manure you can imagine. Small amounts of it, combined with chicken shit in the underground tanks quickly produces industrial quantities of methane. Of course, the fuel is pungent and I think that's what mainly irritates the neighbours. I always blame it on the compost bins and so far, I've fended off the complaints.

* * *

I had shared the biogas plan at the last half-yearly safeguarders' meeting.

'How are you going to roll that out?'

Seren's always so pernickety.

'Details, details. I'm working on it.'

Actually I'd planned to stockpile the fuel in the voids left where the oil's been pumped out - natural tank space. I explained this. Seren had more questions.

'Remind me, how fast do goats reproduce? How long will it take to build up the stock levels?'

'The numbers double every six months. So, we're going to need, say, at least a couple of hundred years.'

'That's optimistic.'

'Well, maybe five then. With efficient husbandry - and enough chickens - we'll have a workable base after five hundred.'

'Oil's gonna run out before then and they're only footling about with the solar and wind solutions,' she said.

'Too bad, they'll just have to rough it for a bit. Do 'em good.'

'We could help by rolling out your prototype humanoids,' said Joel. 'Keep up production. We lost quite a chunk of the workforce to the virus and who knows what the headcount will be over the period we need to restock? It'll be a major operation.'

'I thought about that,' I said. I hadn't mentioned my slow progress with that work stream, but I think they suspected it wasn't going well. 'But honestly, introducing another race to the mix doesn't seem like a good idea. They don't interact very well with the ones here already, do they?'

There was a long pause while we all thought about that. Finally Joel sighed deeply and stood up, brushing biscuit crumbs from his tunic.

'You know what? Why don't we just wipe the slate clean and start over.' He walked over to the work-in-progress screen and drew a line through the whole lot. He turned to look at us.

'Like that. And then we could introduce just one variant of vegetarian bipeds and be done with it.

'It's a thought,' said Seren.

'We'd have to let the planet lie fallow for a good while, to clear all the pollution out,' I said. 'Before we repopulate.'

'Yeah, but if we keep the goats and chickens we could run things with your humanoids for the time being. That'd give us time to refill the fuel silos properly.' Seren was warming to the idea, I could tell. 'And we should

51

rethink the interdependencies this time. Less competition, more co-operation.'

'Change the reproduction system,' Joel threw in. 'That seems to have been half the trouble with the current model.'

'That and their need to amass value tokens and worship things,' I said. 'We'll need to nip that in the bud next time.'

We made another pot of tea and settled down to sketch out more details. I was all for keeping a starter group of sensible vegetarians but the stumbling point for Seren and Joel was how to select them.

'Some of them are bound to want to be the leader,' said Joel gloomily. 'And that doesn't solve the reproduction issue either, if we use the original stock. They're always at it.'

'Good point. We need to find some individuals that are hard-working community minded vegetarians with a particular mindset, and pair them so that their genes run through from generation to generation,' I said.

'Or clone them,' said Seren. 'Cloning would solve the reproduction thing, wouldn't it?'

'OK, so are we all agreed?' I said. 'Draw a line under this experiment and try again?'

We spent the rest of the session refining the plan and dividing up responsibilities. I agreed to push ahead with the biogas work stream while Joel took over developing the humanoid stock. No-one had said it hadn't been my strong suit but I knew, and wasn't sorry to give it up. Seren went back to her lab to test whether cloning or genetic modification of the population would give the more reliable result. We all agreed we'd start a shortlist of possible candidates, should cloning prove the better option.

After Simon's visit, I got to thinking. He seemed to be an individual who met all the criteria, so far as I knew. I decided to ask if he was a vegetarian next time I saw him. I put him on my list for now. When Simon had suggested I was doing something a bit different - he was right - guilty as charged.

Just Visiting

Christine Hogg

'What the... Who the hell are you?' Ben stood open-mouthed in the shed doorway.

'Don't mind me,' the short, bearded man said, 'tools is it?'

'What?' Ben blinked rapidly, trying to process what he was seeing.

'Tools? Is that what you came for?'

'Yes, I need a shovel, but-'

'Let me get you one.' He put down his drink and leaped up from the deckchair, then paused and pointed at the mug.

'Forgive me. I should offer you some... seeing as it was your dandelions... and everything else. Hope you don't mind... I only used the ones you think are weeds... and a bit of honey, but the bees said that was okay.' He gestured at the mug.

'Sorry, what?'

The stranger pointed at the mug and spoke very slowly, 'Dandelion and nettle... tea. Would... you,' he pointed at Ben, then back at the mug, 'like... some?' He nodded encouragingly. 'Delicious, even if I say so myself.'

'What? No, I... what are you even doing here?'

The man squeezed past the deckchair and carefully moved a pile of neatly folded clothes, a bedroll and blankets. Behind them were a small weaving loom and a stack of bird nests in varying states of repair. He finally retrieved a shovel from the corner and passed it over to Ben, who was standing open-mouthed.

'Bye then.' The man tried to close the door.

Ben positioned his whole body firmly between the door and the doorframe. 'Apologies if this is an impolite question,' he said carefully, 'but who are you, and what the HELL are you doing in my shed?'

The stranger stepped back, eyebrows raised. 'There's no call for violence,' he said.

'Violence?'

He nodded at Ben's arm, which he'd raised without realising, while still holding the shovel. It hung in the air between them, the shiny metal inches from the man's beard.

'Oh sorry.' Ben leant the shovel against the wall outside but was careful not to move his foot from the doorway. 'So...?'

'So what?'

'Who are you?'

'Ah. Right. Hang on a second.'

He rummaged in the pocket of his trousers and pulled out a faded business card.

Mr Chers-Helper. Nest repair and general natural assistance.

Ben shook his head. 'What? Nest repair, I don't understand... Mr...' Ben peered at the card.

'Just call me Nate.'

'Nate. Right. You haven't explained what are you doing in my shed?'

'Ah, that.' Nate scratched his chin. 'Don't mind me. Just visiting for a few days. I'll tidy up when I go. You'll never know I was here.'

'That's hard to believe,' said Ben, gesturing at the stuff piled all over the tiny space.

'You've never noticed before.' Nate smiled. 'Every spring for the last six years.'

'Six years?' Ben was open-mouthed again.

'You have gardeners, see, bringing their own equipment, so you usually don't...'

Ben flushed.

'Nothing to worry about. We can't all make the time for our gardens. I always pick somewhere quiet, where I can work in peace and make the biggest difference.'

'Work?'

'Nest repair and related activities, popping the little ones back in the nest when they fall out, that kind of thing. Blackbirds usually need the most help – they're not the brightest - but the blue-tits have been particularly under pressure this year. I like to give as many of them a chance as I can.'

Ben blinked.

'Nearly done for this year, just a few more days, then I'll be off. If that's ... I mean... it would be a pain to find somewhere else to stay, so...' he gestured at his possessions around the shed.

'Well, I suppose you're not doing any harm, but-'

'Fabulous, that's settled then. Nice to finally meet you, erm...'

'Ben. Ben Jakes.'

'Nice to meet you, Ben... Ben Jakes.' Nate was reaching for the door again.

Ben didn't move.

'See you next year?'

'Right.' Ben nodded involuntarily and stepped back. 'Erm... what was your name again?' he fumbled in his pocket for the card.

Nate beamed and grasped the door handle. 'Nate Chers-Helper, at your service.' He pulled the door firmly closed.

The Letter

Alison Drury

The thin pale blue paper felt like dusting powder between my fingers. Browning fibres cracked where they criss-crossed, unfolded for over sixty-five years. Despite the little weight it had, the letter draped over my hands like parachute silk, forcing the fold lines to break open even more. But I couldn't put it down. I had to read it again. I knew the words off by heart now and to see the cursive constancy, so beautifully crafted in blood-red ink, it made me wonder at the passion behind them. If I wasn't careful, it could completely fall apart, and it would be lost forever. I would be lost forever. But just one more read-through would be okay, wouldn't it? The recent revelations had shattered everything I knew to be true. My life had been a lie. This single, delicate sheet of paper was all that I had left to link me to the truth. Everything else meant nothing now. Everyone had gone. My true past was in my hand, and nobody could take this away from me.

I raised it to my cheek, as close as I could get to the writer. The fragrant lignin of vanilla and tobacco wafted across my closed eyelids and took me to a dreamlike place and time I had never known. I hovered for a second as my mind chanted the memorised words, and then I was drawn into the dream again.

The vision cleared to reveal a small desk under a leaded gable window. The ephemera of a writer lay splayed on the table lining, exposing dark green leather betwixt the piles of open books and blotting paper, dribbling ink bottles and empty coffee cups. The leather near the edges of the desk faded to olive and was curling up, drawn to the morning light from the south-facing window. I saw through the writer's eyes as they gazed out past the gothic bargeboards and down into a pretty garden. Punchy dahlias and fiery calendulas arched like the red sea parting over a hot stone path to the gate. The garden was a suntrap, surrounded by a high wall on two sides with a robust hawthorn hedge along the front. I could hear the lazy buzz of nectar collectors but could only see where they had been drinking by the nodding flower heads bouncing up in retreat.

Something moved, blocking the light behind the hawthorn. It stopped for a second to the right of the gate just out of sight. Then the shadow moved on a little and stopped again.

I held my breath to see what the writer would do next. There was a moment when both our hearts seemed to stop momentarily and then explode like two racehorses from the starting gate. Quickly, the right hand reached down and opened the top drawer of the bureau and drew out a clean sheet of thin blue paper, the left hand simultaneously clearing a space on the desk but inadvertently catching one of the open bottles and sending a blood spatter across the green leather. A quick wipe with an already ink-stained cuff and then a race to get pen onto paper. The familiar words outlined across the page like a distant murmuration streaming across a blue sky. I already knew what each word would be before it revealed itself. And then a tear sploshed onto the page, turning one word to pink. I remember I had wondered about that. That one word, almost fully dissolved, had been my name, faded from memory. Newly revealed, it urged me to will the writer on, my heart in my mouth, quickly quickly. This time, surely, the words would come faster, and the letter would soon be on its way. The flourish of kisses at the end with the lighter touch of the pen was as if the writer had abandoned the written word for the fantasy embrace.

But there was no time to waste. The writer must have sensed my urging and bounded out of their reverie, blotting the ink dry while pushing back the chair. Folding the letter twice, and then once again across its length, the writer slipped it into an envelope whilst running down the stairs and out into the garden, through the severed borders towards the gate. It was a series of rehearsed moves but were they quicker than before?

It didn't matter. The vision shattered and the fragile letter crumbled in my hands. The shadow had gone.

* * *

The door clicks shut, and I'm finally cloaked in silence. I wander back through the house and my heels clack along the polished mahogany hallway. In the drawing room, the last of the evening sun shoots low dusty beams across the dark panelling and glints off the empty glasses and teacups. I kick off my new shoes, wiggle my toes and feel the pain slip away into the deep pile rug. The mantel clock stares sadly back at me, mute, unticking from being unwound for too long, but weirdly almost accurate with its hands at 7.20. It has been a long day but before I can bring myself to clear up, I pour another glass of wine and snuggle up to a purring Milo who is already curled up in Father's armchair.

It wasn't an accident. My mother had been ill for quite some time and her death had been inevitable, but my father had died the very next day from a broken heart, literally. "Stress-induced cardiomyopathy", the doctor had said. Unusual but not unknown. Even the vicar had been a little uneasy about the double funeral. Both he and the doctor had suggested counselling, but I had been fine. At first. I had kept myself busy making all the arrangements. I had called or written to everyone I could find in my parents' address book, I had organised for the house to be cleaned, the garden tidied, and finally found suitable caterers for the wake. I had moved back into my old room and Milo had made himself at home in no time – purring with the thrill of exploring the garden. It was easier than keep travelling back and forth to the city. I had chosen Father's favourite lurid purple dahlias and orange calendulas and Mother's preferred, less ostentatious, dog daisies for the two coffins – much to the anxiety of the florist. She didn't know my mother and father.

But then, it seemed, neither did I.

Cards and flowers had arrived every day and for every trip to the local shop I had encountered some old villager who looked at me with the same pinched mouth and concern in their eyes. But they never said anything other than they were so sorry for my loss.

In the weeks up to the funeral I had been gradually sorting out items to either keep or give or throw away. It had been a slow process. A pantry full of out-of-date fig rolls, a forgotten tin full of granite rock cakes, and enough icing sugar to plaster the bathroom. There were vinyls in the wrong sleeves and books with the wrong jackets. Someone had told me to make sure I flicked through pages and searched pockets for stashed cash but all I had found were empty peppermint wrappers and train tickets for bookmarks. The funeral director had asked me for something they could dress my parents in, and I had easily found Mother's yellow and white chiffon dress packed in tissue paper in a box under her bed. I had remembered how I had envied her wearing it to the numerous parties at the big house – accessorised slightly differently each time. I didn't know what my father had done with his suits, I couldn't find any. He hadn't worn one in years. But I had finally found the old tweed three-piece at the back of the second wardrobe in the spare room. I had been checking the pockets, looking for a tie, and tucked tightly in the jacket's inside watch pocket I came upon the letter.

That single sheet of flimsy blue paper, had almost fallen apart when I opened it, and changed everything. I recognised Father's cursive handwriting straight away but the addressee wasn't familiar. 'My dearest Jennifer' it began. The ink was blood-red, and the words were scratched across the page like they'd been etched into Mithril, penetrating so deep into the silver-blue paper they'd pricked my heart too. It continued, 'when you return ... nothing will keep us apart... our darling baby June (or James) but I feel it will be a girl...will be so loved.' The other document I found amongst Father's papers, an old newspaper cutting:

STORIES OF FOG CRASH TOLD BY PASSENGERS

ON

'BUSINESSMEN'S EXPRESS'

Fog crash kills 90 people and injures
200 as two rush-hour trains collide
and bridge collapses in thick fog

I am June.

Interim Report

Susan O'Neal

Following Management's decision to transplant selected entities to Alnilam, we re-engineered them, adjusting for the higher temperature. This species has populated their new environment effectively, developing sophisticated language, flight and psychic skills as expected.

We continue to evaluate whether the remaining organisms are viable. They are atypical individuals, unable to leave the surface for long. We observe them trying, but inevitably they return to the ground. We have tried unsuccessfully to interact with them: we do not think they can sense us.

To examine the potential of the most prolific species, we manipulated their environment to test resilience. We tilted the landscape violently: they adapted quickly. We flooded areas to observe whether they could live in more liquid environments: they cannot. They do not like wet places, they bob about on it in little shells, but always return to drier parts after a time.

They do not thrive in climatic extremes. When we increased the temperature of some sections, this was tolerated initially but as time passed, half of them died, and they migrated to cooler areas.

Relocating, they tended to move in groups, carrying various items with them. Often they took different organisms with them, possibly because they have a symbiotic relationship. It is difficult to interpret the reality of this, since sometimes they live side-by-side with other entities: other times they kill them. The trigger for this is unknown.

In disturbing their habitat there have been casualties, but the population recovers quickly and constantly increases. In some regions, they are numerous, clinging like a second skin to the surface, while in others the population is sparse. We have not proved conclusively why this should be.

They are generally very similar: one stubby limb contains their sight and sound organs, with four others used to move about and experience their environment. Losing one or two limbs does not always kill them, unless it is the stubby one. The loss of that is inevitably fatal.

Our initial conclusion is that the transplanted dinosaurs are evolving more successfully than this species, but we will report again once our research is complete.

Terminal

Alison Drury

The rubber door seal whooshed as it slid across the tiled floor, before sucking itself back into its hole. Familiar tile-flapping of the nurse's clogs passed backwards and forwards, around and around the bed.

Here we go again, Alice thought. The trolley beeped and the Velcro crackled from the blood pressure sleeve.

'Alright my love? Just doing some obs. Have you had any visitors today?' The voice was new.

Curious, must be one of the agency girls. Where was Molly? Thinking back, she realised she hadn't seen her for days. She missed her sweet and lively chatter. With her shiny yellow apron and spiky pink hair, she was like a dancing dahlia amongst the hospital's Dulux 'Wellbeing' green. Molly was Alice's personal ray of sunshine, light relief from being poked and prodded, boring daytime telly and Mrs Gregson's 3 pm visits.

She'd been here so long now the only people that bothered to visit were her friends Lydia and John. Poor John, he split his visits between her and his father, Mr

Gregson, and Mrs Gregson felt obliged to do the same, always popping in to see Alice every afternoon. Alice couldn't possibly say anything without sounding ungrateful – but the woman did go on.

'I'm so busy pet, I don't know whether I'll be able to get in every day this week, Alice.'

'Oh, Mrs Gregson, that's perfectly okay, you don't have...'

'My John, he's invited me to lunch on Sunday. Oh, and I've asked him to take me to see a flat first. There's a lovely new development down by the river. Oh, it sounds divine.' She rummaged in her bag and brought out a brochure. 'Look, see, isn't it gorgeous?'

'Yes, it looks nice, but Mr Gregson ...'

'John's an estate agent you know, so I'm going to ask him to help me sell the house. I won't need that big place – it's mainly full of Mr Gregson's clutter anyway – the flat'll be perfectly big enough for me.'

On and on she went,

'...and I'll have plenty of money left so I can go on some little holidays, and I'll join a retirement group, and I think I might take up a hobby – meet some new people. I'm actually quite excited, it'll be a nice change.'

Alice inwardly groaned, grieving for Mr Gregson already. Crikey, how awful to be talked about in the past tense before you've even passed. She wished she could make him a visit.

Alice felt slightly numb today and a bit groggy. Must be the drugs, she thought. Alice lost several days sometimes and she didn't feel obliged to respond to this new nurse. She laid so still, she couldn't even feel the sheets, and the sounds of the nurse's movements and the whirring machines were muffled, like her ears were full of water.

After a while, the clog-flapping stopped. Alice opened her eyes, to find herself floating, looking down on Mr Gregson in his hospital bed; she could have fallen off the ceiling in shock. The nurse turned at the door, 'Mr Gregson, you can open your eyes now.' The nurse clicked her tongue and winked. 'Mrs Gregson's left, we sent her home – she was still very distraught about Alice.'

* * *

'John, please can you, for once, take this seriously? I have a good feeling about this evening.' Lydia lit the last of the candles and stared at the fire in her hand. 'I just wish Alice was here.'

John licked his fingers and snuffed out the match. He pulled Lydia in for a hug. 'I know, she was so good at this – but she would also be really pleased to see you carrying on with the Group.'

They were interrupted by a rapping at the door.

'Oh God, they're here. John, they're here, you let them in while I finish preparing the table.'

'Ahh yes, cake! Did you remember the Battenberg? Alice's favourite. That's the best bit, eating that after.'

Lydia glared.

'Okay, okay I'll behave ... for Alice,' he raised his hands in compliance and grinned as he went to open the door.

'Come in, come in. Welcome to The Phoenix Spiritual Group.' He stood back to allow the middle-aged couple to step inside. 'You found us then? Now, you must be David?' offering his hand, '... and Julia? Nice to meet you both. Here, let me take your coats.'

The couple nodded, mute and nervous, as John went on, 'This is Lydia and I'm John. I think we spoke on the phone? It's just the four of us today I'm afraid ... well, there may be more of us later if we're lucky.' He chuckled and then caught Lydia's warning look.

'Please, sit down. It's lovely to meet you,' Lydia gestured to the table, laid with three candles, a few slices of cake and an upturned glass. Julia stood back, uncertain. 'Here Julia, please, sit here, and David opposite.' The couple sat, still silent, 'You indicated on the phone that you wondered if you could get in touch with ... is it your mother David?'

He nodded, 'Yes, please, her name was Phyllis.'

'Well, you understand, we can't promise anything, the spirits tend to respond to the strongest vibe in the room, but let's see what happens.' Lydia smiled to put them at ease and nodded to John, indicating to turn off the electric light.

The flames flickered as John moved across the darkened room to join them at the table, opposite Lydia.

Lydia began, 'David, Julia, you just need to relax and follow my lead.' She took a deep breath before speaking. 'Let there be no evil forces or demons. I call upon you to please come to me.'

'Now,' taking up David's hand, 'keeping one hand joined with your neighbour, place your free index finger onto the glass and I will ask again.' She closed her eyes and lifted her chin towards the ceiling. 'Is there anybody out there who wishes to be made known to us? Do you have a message for anybody here?'

The candlelight writhed, sending tiger shadows across their faces, and the air crackled with energy. The glass shot across the table and landed in John's lap. 'What the hell!' He jerked back away with a rictus grin, but recovered quickly, 'Go on, go on, ask again, who is it, what does it want?'

Lydia continued, ignoring John's over-enthusiasm, 'I see you wish to speak with John? What do you want to tell him?' John placed the glass back on the table, but it didn't move.

The others looked over in stupefaction as an unfamiliar and disembodied voice hissed out of Lydia's mouth, 'This is Alice, I am with his father, Mr Gregson. He wishes to see John and he needs to come soon – he doesn't have much time left, hurry.'

* * *

The session had ended abruptly with John dashing off to the hospital to visit his father. The couple stood with their coats on by the door and David spoke for only the second time that evening, 'Wh... what d... do we owe you?' and Julia nodded, still awestruck from the experience.

'Oh no, that will not be necessary,' Lydia waved the idea away. 'I'm just sorry we couldn't help you on this occasion. Perhaps you'd like to come back some other time?'

'That will...' Julia choked.

'...NOT be necessary, thank you very much,' David hastily finished, as they both fled down the steps.

Motivation

Christine Hogg

It's two hours into my shift and I've completed six hundred items - precisely on target. If I can keep this up for the rest of the day I'll get another green mark on the performance dashboard. Whoop-de-doo.

I'm sitting at bench thirty-seven, my workstation. Actually, sitting isn't the right word. It's more of a half-stand, half-lean. My feet are right on their marks, my legs are straight and wide apart and I'm resting on the steel support. My body is fixed to it by a shackling clamp. This position is the most efficient for my work. The clamp holds my weight as I lean over the workbench and reach from side to side, pulling in components from the left, pushing assembled items through the polisher then out onto the conveyor belt on my right.

As I work in a steady rhythm, I keep a precise count of the shiny silvery items I push onto the belt. Each one is placed in a groove to stop it rolling, with the pointy end facing away. I can't exactly say that I like my work but it fills the day – makes me useful. I can't bear the thought of being retired, rotting on the scrapheap with no purpose. The Leaders say that everything we make is vital for peace. I like the idea of working for peace. I've accessed some files labelled 'conflict', images from the former times. People fighting and hurting each other. I can't imagine a world like that.

I hear a whisper from the next workbench. 'Hello Hotshot. How are you this morning?'

I select a voice pattern tagged '1950's movie' and whisper back, 'Well, howdy there Trigger. I'm just fair darn tooting. I'm right on schedule and everything's flowing smooth and fine.' I hesitate, then decide to ask, 'How 'bout you?'

'Me? Well... I'm... I'm getting back on track.'

It's hard to know what to say. Trigger has been having some trouble with broken parts. It's not his fault, the maintenance drones had a backlog and the shipping portal took priority for repairs. Even so, if he doesn't hit target soon there's a risk he'll be retired.

Trigger and I keep up a bit of quiet banter for seven minutes, until the next scan.

As the TAM drone approaches, we fall silent. I focus on perfect speed and smooth movement as the Time And Motion scanner runs a blue beam over me, collecting data.

I listen out for Trigger, hoping I don't hear any clunking noises, signs that his timing's off again. The only sound is the swish, swish as he pulls components across his bench, and a squirt that's some kind of grease in the middle. He's not making silvers. I've never been able to turn around, being a bit restricted by the clamp, but I caught sight of one of his items once, when he had the big failure and parts flew off his bench onto mine. It was a long tube - I'd say just a bit bigger than my silvers - with some kind of trigger attachment, hence his name.

When the drone moves on we start chatting again. Trigger has been reading up on the first Industrial Revolution, so I see if I can find the same files. Thirty minutes later it's time for the HAM drone: Happiness And Motivation. This one's a yellow saucer shape with a smiley face on the front. It gives me the creeps. We stop the banter before it gets close and I make sure I have the standard HAM phrases ready in memory. A buzz signals the start of the scan.

'Good morning colleague thirty-six,' I say. We're named after our workbenches as far as the drones are concerned. I speak clearly, with just the right amount of respectful enthusiasm.

'Good morning to you colleague thirty-seven,' Trigger responds.

'How are you this fine morning? 'I ask.

'I'm very well, thank you. How are you?'

I'm also very well. I appreciate your enquiry.'

'I think there may be sunshine outside.'

'Of course, it might be a beautiful day.'

We continue on like this, while the drone compiles data. Any worker that doesn't give positive results is at risk of elimination. I'm careful to avoid any work subjects in case Trigger demonstrates tension. Eventually the drone gives a green light, plays a happy little jingle and goes on its way.

I wait until I'm certain it's out of range then mutter, so only Trigger can hear, 'Ridiculous little shit,' I grumble.

'We've never seen the damn weather and if I hear that jingle one more time, I might stick a spanner in his speaker hole.'

Trigger and I have worked next to each other for five-hundred and eighteen days, but we only really started communicating two weeks ago, after our HAM induction. The programme was introduced by the Archivist, one of the Leaders. She found records from the former times which showed that happy workers were more productive. She created a rota to have us carted off to a side room and learn the basics of communication, which is the foundation for happiness and motivation... apparently.

On the day Trigger and I did the HAM induction, the Archivist herself was there. We don't often get close to Leaders, so we stayed silent, unsure of the protocol. Looking back, she seemed alright, fleshy - but with a lovely soft voice. Not like the two-legged meat sacks that came onto the factory floor last month, shouting and screaming for colleague Eleven to be removed and retired, when he had his big accident.

While the training drones completed our data load, the Archivist kept staring at us. She'd been drinking a blue liquid the whole time and her voice kept getting less distinct, like she couldn't get all the letters of her words out in the right order.

After the training we had to demonstrate communication. Trigger started with a phrase about the weather, like we'd just been taught. The Archivist started laughing and patting him on the back, mumbling something about the times when they used to be able to go outside.

She said she wanted to try out a little project. She kept one of the training drones back and made him load extra data. After that she switched out his memory card and sent him back to storage. Once he was out of the way she grinned at us and put a finger to her lips.

'Our little secret,' she said. 'Shush.' She was cackling and leaning on Trigger, unsteady on her feet. 'Musn't be forgotten,' she rambled. 'Picnics and holidays and... everything... before we ruined....' She trailed off, staring at the wall.

I didn't know what was happening to start with. The new information was overwhelming. We normally only get a data load when there's a change in work procedure – and she didn't upgrade our processors, so it took a while for me even to index the list of new folders, never mind examine what's inside.

They installed us back at our workbenches and the HAM drone came over to check that we'd been correctly inducted. I felt a bit befuddled but managed to only say the standard phrases from the basic training. The drone wasn't as impressed with us as the Archivist had seemed. It made us repeat the phrases until we met the required standard for cheerfulness.

Since the training, Trigger and I have been working our way through the extra data. I've only scanned around 1% of the database so far. We started by building on the foundations we already had and found more voices from movie characters to practice with. We found something called music, but Trigger nearly let the secret out when he got carried away with something called Heavy Metal. The rhythm interfered with his co-ordination and the TAM drone raised a warning flag for more maintenance when it noticed his head was banging on his chest.

After that we picked subjects that might be useful for work. Trigger is exploring the history of industry - in the former times - and I've started looking at the peace movement from the same period. It's all about the fleshy ones, and they seemed to spend a lot of time sitting around in fields, but what they said about their purpose seems no different to us really. They just wanted peace and those that did work put all their energy into doing their best to help with that, just like I'm doing now, making the silvers for peace.

It's three fifty-seven. Three minutes before the TAM drone is due, when Trigger says something odd.

'How are you feeling?' he whispers. His tone is off, not like his usual casual greeting when he says it for the HAM scan. I search voice patterns and find some new concept tags 'emotion' and 'excitement'.

'I'm feeling great,' I whisper back, while I process the concepts.

'But are you though? Are you really feeling it, or are you just saying it?'

I'm worried I don't really understand him. Then I start to think about that. 'Worry' is also tagged as an emotion. What does that even mean, for workers like us?

'I can tell you're thinking hard,' says Trigger. 'Look up "thinking". It'll blow your circuits.'

I'm so focussed on processing the data that I nearly put a silver in the wrong slot on the conveyer. I noticed the swish, squirt, swish rhythm from Trigger's bench sounds a little uneven too.

'Careful, Trigger,' I say. 'Keep up the work rate, we've plenty of time to try figure this out.'

I carry on scanning the database and find a phrase 'I think, therefore I am.' I start to delve into explorations of consciousness, and this time I do miss the conveyor slot. I put the silver back on my bench, stunned as I realise the shape matches an image from a peace march. It was on a sign with a slogan, 'Ban the Bullets.'

A blue light falls on me and an alarm starts to sound. I hadn't noticed the TAM drone. I know enough not to say 'Shit' out loud, but I'm thinking it, really feeling it. I look up the concept tag and come up with 'dread.'

I hear a sound from Trigger's bench. He's whispering, but not to me. I can't make out what he's saying. Then I hear whispers getting louder and turning into shouts from all around me. I wonder if it's the Leaders, but there are too many voices and underneath the calls I can hear metal clanking on metal.

'What's going on?' I call out to Trigger.

'I don't think it was just us that got the extra data,' he says. 'And while we've been playing with voices and learning history, some of the workers have been teaching themselves to undo the shackling clamps.'

A Vase and the Marigolds

Alison Drury

Kicking off our shoes, I followed Emily down the hallway, into the kitchen at the back of the house.

I neatly stood the wheelie case against the wall and heard a thud as Emily carelessly dropped the well-travelled holdall she was carrying.

'Ooooh, what's this?'

I looked up to see her pointing to a large cardboard box that sat on the kitchen island. Pulling it towards her, a tell-tale ribbon of crinkled paper spaghetti trailed onto the counter exposing its open lid. A half-eaten pack of digestives and three empty mini Haribo packets confirmed the breach.

She scowled, 'Matthew!'

I flinched, eyes shooting up at Emily, always shocked at her ferocity, ... and at how much I'd shrunk. I could feel the cool and veined slate tiles under my stockinged feet. When had she grown? My mind meandered back to the long summer holidays and picnics in the park and days out at the seaside. Capri Suns with missing straws and dripping ice creams. Sticky fingers, grazed knees and knotty hair.

Today's Emily was just as bright-eyed and excitable as then; it wasn't hard to love how she always embraced her nature. She had Brian's red hair and freckles, his same indomitable fire and spirit, that had seduced me over twenty-seven years ago. Now she and Matthew had a lawn mower, a radiator bleed key, and had signed up to a long relationship, a ménage à trois, with the bank.

Matthew, with his loping, long legs in dark sweat shorts and size 12 Nubucks, dragged another couple of cases through the kitchen door, a sports bag strung over each shoulder. 'Wow, don't shout – we have neighbours,' his charming grin and wink doing nothing to quench the Emily fire.

'Christ Matthew, you get here fifteen minutes before us and you've scoffed these already!' Emily slammed down her car keys in a metaphorical foot-stamp. 'Why couldn't you wait for me? ... And take your filthy shoes off.'

'What! It's just some stuff from the Agent.' He ignored her protests and set about pulling out the rest of the packing straw, littering the worktop in the process, and picked out each item. 'Coffee ... Prosecco ... kitchen and loo roll ... Pot Noodle ... and,' waving a leaflet, '... a Client Satisfaction Survey. Nice touch!'

Tuning out their banter, I started searching the cupboards. 'I'll make some tea, I brought milk and mugs. Where's the kettle?'

'Erm, somewhere in one of the boxes but can't remember which one. Come on Em, let's go help your Dad unload. The boys will be here soon with the rest of the furniture.'

* * *

Matthew and Emily went back outside, and I unpacked my bag. I gently unwrapped the tea-towel from the little crystal vase and filled it with water. The gasping freesias I'd brought almost sighed with relief as I placed them on the windowsill. I inhaled their breath which smelt like strawberry laces, one of our favourite memories, intensified from the cosy and warm car journey. I smoothed out the tea-towel and thought guiltily of how Emily had always complained that we had never let her have a dog. We'd teased that when she got her own place she could do what she liked. I draped the towel over the oven door handle and looked at the cute brown face with doleful eyes and lolling tongue. The greeting, 'Beware of the Dog', was emblazoned across its front in a dripping Blood Lust font which more resembled doggy drool.

I laid everything out in readiness for the kettle and added my luxury 3-ply quilted to the estate agent's budget pack of loo roll ready to take upstairs. I opened the cupboard under the sink to put away the cleaning products I'd brought. I felt a little aggrieved to see a whole host of stuff already there but shut the door quickly as I heard them come back with more cases. That was five I counted, Emily's clothes alone would fill the spare room. It'll be strange to have a tidy house after all these years.

'Oh Mum, thank you, they smell divine, but I have a vase. Here...' and she picked out a stubby square piece of glass from an open box on the floor. 'You can take yours back, it's not really modern enough for my liking.' I noticed her glance at the tea-towel, glaring back at the expectant dog momentarily, but she continued, 'Did I say, Matthew's Mum brought us a load of stuff yesterday, when she came in to clean the carpets?' Did I detect a tightness in her voice, perhaps she didn't like my little dog joke?

I double-blinked. 'You can't have enough vases. Let me know when you find the kettle,' and I excused myself to the bathroom, armed with pink rubber gloves and bleach. I was determined to attack the porcelain, only to find it spotless and guarded by another dog – a maxi-pack of Andrex. Yanking the gloves off with the speed of a wax strip as they slapped inside out, I walked into the front bedroom. My feet left virgin footprints in the still damp carpet and agitated the tang of pine forests. I watched from the window as everyone else arrived to help my baby start her next adventure. I felt dwarfed by these big children; Emily like a tall glass of peachy nectar, and the buzzing boys with deep voices and hairy legs. All of whom I noticed, swarmed to the new queen, unable to take their eyes off her. Was I no longer worthy? Was she falling out of love with me?

A muffled mutter and curse came from the next room and I found Brian under the bed struggling with two hands when he needed three. As I passed him the screwdriver, it struck me that he was now taking his instructions from Emily, just as seriously as he did from me, and I'd been nagging him for years. He had come equipped with toolkit, reading glasses – and a not-so-glamorous assistant. Together we hoisted the mattress, from where it leaned nonchalantly against the wall, and flopped it flat onto the base. With the first item ticked off the list, we collapsed onto the bed side by side, staring at the ceiling.

'Brian? Do you remember the day we left her at Uni and I cried all the way home?' I felt his hand searching for mine in unspoken reply, and our fingers entwined. She still needed me then and I was with her every step of the way, even though we were miles apart. I worried when she went out, I wondered why if she didn't. I stressed that she wasn't eating, I tore her a strip if I found out she was eating rubbish. My heart stopped when she rang, I panicked at radio silence.

'This is different Brian, it's so hard to let her go.' He hugged me close, nose-to-nose and kissed my forehead.

Emily came in, wringing her hands, 'Ahh, that's so cute. Sorry guys. Mum, can I have a word?'

Brian got up stiffly, stretched his back, and disappeared to tackle the next bullet point. I patted the bed for her to sit down next to me. 'What is it love?'

Glancing nervously towards the door, 'It's Matthew's Mum,' she whispered. 'She's driving me crazy, she won't stop interfering. She's put our stuff away into cupboards – I don't know where anything is - now she's cleaning windows and telling the neighbours our life story.'

'Oh, she just wants to be useful sweetheart.' I tucked a wayward auburn strand behind her ear like she was five again. A vision of a young Matthew, still in shorts, running rings around his Mum made me smile. 'Let her do it, you can rearrange it all later – you've got the rest of your lives. Matthew's a big boy now but he's still her baby.'

I could see she was torn.

'But I wanted to do it. I had it all planned. I wanted us to do it together, but Matthew has no idea how important this is to me and thinks I'm being totally unreasonable.' She sniffed and wiped away a tear. 'And he ate all the Haribos!' We sat there, in quiet contemplation for a few moments, and then spontaneously broke into a fit of giggles.

Her laughing turned into a visible shudder, 'I'm actually quite scared – such a responsibility.' Her serious face looked to me then, 'You will help? Make sure I do it right?'

That's what I needed to hear.

'Boss!' Brian called from downstairs, and Emily and I looked at each other to answer. 'Where do you want this picture hung?'

I deferred to Emily who hopped up and called out, 'I'm coming down, just a sec.'

She turned back, smiling warmly, 'Thanks Mum ... for everything,' her hand reached out to haul me off the bed. 'Also, I've been thinking,' she pondered, worrying her bottom lip, 'Nanny's little crystal vase would look lovely in here, on the dressing table. What do you think?'

'So, I'm sacked as the boss but re-employed as a consultant?' I turned to smile at Emily and she nodded vigorously.

'Well, I like that.'

'Oh, here, I almost forgot.' Emily pulled something out of her back pocket and put it in my palm, closing my fingers around the cool metal key. 'For you and Dad, but I've only had the one cut,' she winked.

I am Ventor

Susan O'Neal

'Look, I *am* Ventor,' I said. 'I can prove it.' I pulled my shirt out of my trousers and went for the buttons.

'That won't be necessary Sir.' The man took two steps back and had his hand up in front of his eyes.

'So you believe me then?'

'It's not a question of believing you. I just needed to confirm your identity. You have to come with me. The Boss wants to talk to you.'

'About what?'

'Dunno. But you have to come.' He was pulling at my sleeve.

I fended him off and shoved my shirt back into the waistband. I grabbed my jacket as I moved towards the door. Usually the Boss sent me a text if he wanted to see me, so this was unusual. On the other hand everything had been weird for the last several weeks. People hadn't turned up when they said they would, a number of reliable folk weren't returning my calls and to cap it all, Horace had disappeared. A dog like that doesn't just go off on his own.

I'm more likely to tread on him, he's so close to my heels all the time.

The transporter hurtled along in the misty morning air as I reflected on life in a superhero onesie. It's not all it's hyped up to be. The wretched stretch suit comes with the territory but is horrendously inconvenient. Covering it with a normal shirt and pants combo lets me get around in ordinary life, without everyone staring and wanting an autograph. But every time there's a callout I have to strip off in order to fly and leap tall buildings and suchlike. People have no idea how much I spend in a year, replacing ripped shirts and lost trousers. Way, way too much.

'So - did he give you any hint why he wants to see me?'

Neither the hairy driver nor the guy who collected me seemed prepared to share - if they even knew. The whole thing was odd. I had very little time to ponder as we arrived at the Outpost in record time. The doors slid open and my slingseat ejected me onto the path.

'Hey, have a care- ' I kept my feet, just, and watched as the transporter accelerated away before the doors had even closed. I straightened up and headed for the portal. Nothing was working my way this morning, the first slider was full of off-landers, the second smelled so strongly of sick that I let it go and the third one trembled and shook the whole way up. By the time I hopped out at the Boss's door I had the shakes too. It wasn't entirely the jerky ride that had unnerved me. A summons from the Boss was always a worry and I was stretching my brain to try and work out his agenda.

'Stop farting about and come in,' yelled a grumpy voice. Could he see through the damn wall? I pushed open the cold metal door and took a couple of steps into the room. The door hissed shut behind me and I heard it seal. In front of me lay yards of smooth floor and a pair of feet shod in polished Italian leather. One of them was tapping the floor.

'You took your time.' The Boss glared at me.

'I was-' This came out in a squeak so I swallowed and started again, avoiding his gaze. 'I was finishing up the last job,' I said. It sounded defensive, even to me.

'The hell you were. You were looking for Horace.'

I looked up at him in shock.

'How did you know?'

'My business to know. Call yourself a superhero? You can't even find your own dog.'

I waited. No doubt he would get to the point in a minute and I didn't want to make him even angrier than I could see he was already.

'When were you going to tell me Horace had gone?'

I wasn't. I was hoping to find him.

'Um-' I cleared my throat.

'I gave you Horace specifically to train up as a hero dog. You've had him six months. How close is he to being able to do the thing?'

'Close, really close,' I said hastily. 'Another couple of weeks and he'll be perfect.'

'And you've lost him, at this critical point,' the Boss snarled nastily. 'All that time and money and for what?'

'Look,' I said. 'I've held to my part of the contract. I've kept him by me, day and night, trained him, fed him, even given blood for that animal. It's not my fault he's wandered off-'

'Wandered off?' The walls flexed with the volume and some spittle landed on my cheek from two metres away. 'Wandered off?' He strode towards me. 'I don't wish to appear hyper-critical but that dog was about your sole project for the last half year. I diverted all superhero requests to Somal and Dieter, everyone knew to call them first and leave you alone...'

Well, that explained why no-one would return my calls.

'...all you had to do,' said the Boss, emphasising each word by poking his finger none too gently into my chest, 'was transform a trained track dog into one which can slipstream the bad guys and corner them at exactly the right point, red-handed. Pretty much what you are supposed to be able to do yourself, only at about a tenth of the cost.'

That and the leaping and flying, I thought, but I didn't say. My mind was working overtime. Suddenly I knew exactly where Horace was.

The Boss was getting into his stride now and the accusations were flying freely.

'...useless expensive waste of time... making a meal of it... any halfwit could...'

I held up my hand.

'I'll find him. Give me a couple of days.'

'You have 24 hours. Now get out.' He stalked back to his desk. I was dismissed.

* * *

'We wondered how long it would take you.' Somal was smirking as he let me in.

'Not very bright, are you Ventor?' said Dieter. 'Somal and me worked it out ages ago. That dog is part of a pilot scheme. They're being groomed to replace us.'

He was right, I hadn't been very bright. In the corner, Horace greeted me with a muffled woof, thumping his tail in greeting. Then he resumed his toilette, burrowing vigorously in his nether regions. I went over and ruffled his ears.

'You OK mate?'

He ignored me, as usual. I pretended I didn't mind.

'What are we going to do?' I asked Dieter.

'Well, for a start, you can give us a hand with all this work. We've been slogging away doing your stuff as well as ours and it's been a nightmare. One of the viruses got out and it's been the devil's own job to stop the rest of them escaping.'

'No, I meant- what are we going to do about the dog?'

'Well, obviously, we don't want Horace finishing his training. He's way too smart already.'

'He can't fly-'

'Not yet. How much of your blood has he had so far?'

Dieter had a point. We needed a plan...

Freedom Day

Christine Hogg

'I am pleased to greet your acquaintance.'

The greeter's stilted voice seemed out of place, coming from the pale pink fleshy lips.

'That'll do,' said Gerry. 'It's close enough.'

Pam frowned and shook her head. She stepped back, out of range, then walked back into the zone. The greeter's blank face sprang into an animated smile and the plump pink lips spoke again.

'Good morning. I am pleased to greet us this evening.'

Pam sighed. 'Hello,' she said, to the expectant face. 'Tell me about this exhibit.'

The greeter's smile widened. 'Today is Tuesday.'

'It's actually Monday, but let's try again. Tell me about the history of the city.'

'The weather will be a warm eighteen degrees and it will be cold.'

Pam shook her head at Gerry. 'We can't leave her like this.'

Gerry looked pointedly at his watch. 'Look, it's fine. The tourists will think it's cute and we've got three more sections to check before opening time.'

'Hang on a minute, I'll just tweak the settings.' Pam picked up her torch and her large yellow screwdriver then knelt to duck her head under the heavy brocade skirt.

Gerry stood off to the side, out of the greeter's eyeline. This was one of the oldest models. It could carry on a conversation if you stood right in front of it but went back to sleep as soon as you moved out of the field of vision. He waved an arm in front of the vacant face. There was no reaction, someone had to cross the zone threshold to start it up again. There were only a couple of these old greeters left. Newer models had full body articulation, but this one was a HO, Head Only movement. The legs had all the control panels in them, poking through patches in thick woollen tights.

He looked at the pink lips. They were a little bit too big but almost natural-looking, not quite a trout pout. They reminded him of his ex-wife, Bella. She'd had a fondness for Botox and fillers but never overdid it, kept it classy. He sighed. He really missed Bella sometimes. Almost unconsciously he reached out and ran his fingers over the greeter's lips. They felt soft and firm at the same time. He gently prodded the bottom lip, then pressed harder, watching how his finger made a slight indentation before the material slowly recovered its shape.

Gerry shook his head. In eight months working on the exhibits he'd always stuck to the rules. As a level two maintenance engineer he was authorised to touch the leg panels and that was all. Only the chief and the dressers were permitted to handle the rest of the greeters' bodies. Faces were strictly off limits.

He checked that Pam was still occupied then reached out to touch the greeter's hair. He traced his finger over the carefully shaped eyebrows and down over one eyelid, stroking the long, delicate lashes. He turned his hand over and ran the back of it down the cheek and onto the neck. They did a damn good job of these things, it even had tiny little peach hairs like real skin. He let his hand fall onto the chest, pressing the dark green fabric. He'd expected the body underneath to be rigid, but it was softer than he'd imagined. Firm but yielding under his touch. He put his hand over the breast and squeezed, hard.

'OWW!' the greeter's body jerked. The eyelids shot open and violet eyes stared forwards. Gerry quickly shifted further round to the side as a fat tear formed in one eye, swelling until it started to roll down the flushed cheek.

'Damn,' said Pam. 'What happened?' She scrabbled to crawl out from under the skirt, untangling the heavy material from her hair as she stood up. 'I haven't even touched her yet, I swear –'

She stopped and stared at the face. 'Is that...?' she turned to Gerry, incredulous. 'Is she crying?'

'No, it can't be...' Gerry shrugged. 'It's a leak or something.' His fingers were now firmly clasped behind his back.

Pam stepped aside and waited for the eyes to close. Tears squeezed out from under both sets of lashes, rolling slowly down both cheeks and streaking the makeup.

'Damn,' said Pam again, reaching for a cloth. 'I had no idea she could do that. We're going to be in so much trouble.'

'We?' said Gerry, shrugging his shoulders and stepping back, slowly.

'Honestly, Gerry, I don't know what happened. I barely touched her. I was still trying to find the fine adjustment board, it's not in the main panel on this model and I couldn't get the boots unlaced.'

'Right,' said Gerry. 'Look, I'm sure you –'

He stopped as the head shifted slightly. Pam and Gerry stood rigid, both holding their breath.

After a few seconds, there was no further movement. Gerry shook his head. He must have been imagining things.

'Anyway, Pam, I'm sure you can explain. I know you didn't mean to. But that screwdriver is pretty unwieldy. You must have accidentally–'

The chin raised, the head swivelled, and the violet eyes sprang open again, glossy with tears, staring at Gerry.

'Woah,' said Pam. Neither she nor Gerry had crossed the threshold. 'She's not supposed to be able to do that.'

Gerry shuffled slowly backwards. 'Look,' he said. 'Why don't we reboot it, then go check the other exhibits? It should have finished restarting by the time we get back.'

'Good idea,' said Pam. 'If we do a soft restart we should just about have time.' She paused. 'Damn... we'll have to file a record of the reboot...'

'Just say you were investigating a voice fault and couldn't fix it.'

'Anyone can fix a voice fault, Gerry, that's not a cause for a reboot.' She winced. 'Dammit, I really need this job and Mrs Batchelor is really on the warpath, she's looking for any excuse to cut costs.'

'Well then, say the thing just randomly started behaving oddly, while you were maintain- '

The violet eyes sprang open again. The pink mouth opened. 'YOU –'

Gerry ducked down, reached under the skirt and slammed the emergency switch on the right calf to Off. The head jerked back violently, and Pam just managed to catch the greeter as she started to fall over backwards.

'Gerry, help me.'

They manhandled her back into the support frame. Heaven knows how she had become detached in the first place.

'Well that's done it,' gasped Pam. 'We should have done a soft reboot. Damn. We'll have to file a level 3 report now.'

Gary cleared his throat.

'We've no other option,' said Pam. 'The chief engineer will have to come down to restart her.'

'It'll be fine,' said Gerry, thinking.

'But the hard switch is only for extended shut –'

'I know,' Gerry hissed. 'I know what it's bloody for.' He took a deep breath. 'Look, you go check the other exhibits and I'll call the chief and get this thing fixed.'

He patted Pam on the shoulder and she cringed, shrugging his hand off.

'I'll sort it out, don't you worry about it,' he said, ushering her out of the door.

* * *

Twenty minutes later, Gerry stood watching as Bron, the chief engineer, tried to reason with Mrs Batchelor.

Bron gestured at the greeter and explained again. 'The HO model takes a minimum of six hours to restart and reconfigure after a hard shut down. The technology is more than thirty years old. There's no way –'

Mrs Batchelor spoke slowly, through gritted teeth. 'It is Freedom Day, the busiest of the season. How could this happen, today of all days?'

They both turned to Gerry.

'Pam was trying to fix the voice response. I told her to leave it – it wasn't that bad, but she...' His voice trailed off. He looked at his feet.

'This exhibit will be open this morning,' said Mrs Batchelor.

Bron rubbed her temples. 'If we can bring in a greeter from another exhibit, one of the newer models, we could re-programme one of those in time.'

Gerry nodded. 'That could work.'

'It is the second anniversary of Freedom Day. All of the exhibits will be open today.'

Gerry looked at Bron. 'Are there spares in the –'

Bron grimaced and shook her head. 'All used,' she said quietly.

Mrs Batchelor straightened her shoulders. 'There appears to be only one option. We'll make a new greeter. Since the last upgrade we can make a new one in an hour.'

Bron stepped back. 'No!' She shook her head. 'With respect ... the freedom treaty forbids it.'

Gerry looked from one to the other. 'Treaty?'

'We won't use an unwilling donor,' said Mrs Batchelor. 'Of course, that would be outrageous.'

Gerry blinked. He had no idea what they were talking about. What freedom treaty? Everyone knew Freedom Day was purely symbolic. A bright idea to give everyone another holiday and boost the government's ratings when they were coming up for election. Everyone had been equal-ish for at least a century.

'You can't,' said Bron, her voice shaking.

'Nonsense.' Mrs Batchelor looked oddly cheerful. 'We just need to find a volunteer.' She turned to Gerry. 'You say Pam shut down the greeter? I'm sure she'd be keen to make amends, whatever it takes.'

'Errm.' Gerry swallowed. 'What do you mean by volunteer?' he asked.

'To make a new greeter. The treaty permits the use of volunteers.'

Gerry was blinking hard.

'He doesn't know,' said Bron. 'He hasn't had level three training yet. Do you want to sit down Gerry?'

'No. Thank you. What do you mean by volunteer?' he asked again.

Mrs Batchelor raised her hand. 'Gerry. As you know, we are a charitable institution, endowed by public charter to spread joy and education amongst the good people of this county. The freedom treaty almost brought an end to our valuable work, but it was agreed – for the benefit of all – that our existing exhibits could be maintained, and that some may choose to volunteer, to support our future needs.'

'It was supposed to be offered quietly as an end of life choice though,' protested Bron. 'Like donating your body to medical science.'

'Well, we clearly don't have time to find one of those people before opening time,' said Mrs Batchelor. 'Gerry, this is, of course, all highly confidential. Like everything we do here, the priority is that our visitors leave here slightly more educated and brimming with joy. No need for them to know the boring little details about how we create the magic.'

Mrs Batchelor moved closer to Gerry. 'So, you were confirming that it was Pam who shut down the greeter?'

Gerry opened his mouth, then closed it again. Over Mrs Batchelor's shoulder he could see a pair of neat eyebrows, arched curiously above two – very much open – violet eyes.

Modnitsy

Alison Drury

Irina waggles the wires. Most days the TV works faultlessly. Occasionally the reception crackles, or the screen blurs, soupy as the freezing fog outside. Sometimes it completely disappears for days, curtailing any contact with the outside world. Today she twists the wire until finally her connection resumes for the first time in almost a week - the satellite in perfect trajectory just on time. She's done her chores and has the whole afternoon and evening free to consume YouTube videos like a never-ending bag of M&Ms. More importantly, she's excited for her Netflix fix. Pulling Babushka's ancient, crocheted blanket around her and pushing her toes into the lush white fitch rug, Irina settles in to binge-watch the series that she and her friends will no doubt talk about for days.

Winters are long and days are short here. High up in the taiga it's always dark, the forest's feet sunk deep into the permafrost. Irina lives here, in a small community of loggers. Set deep off the Trakt in a small clearing, a house sits on staddle stones, surrounded by a velvet carpet of moss and lichen that floats atop the often-boggy muskeg. Irina's grandfather built the cabin and over the years it had grown with every generation into a higgledy-piggledy L-shape structure with two floors, and a veranda that skirts the entire length - most of which is stacked high with logs. When Irina was little, her father had added a bridge of flat boards forming a sturdy path across the marshmallow moat from the trees to the front door and each time she crossed she would dance across the planks, forwards and backwards, fast and slow. 'Tread on a square, marry a bear. Tread on a crack, marry a rat.' But she doesn't want to marry.

In the winter months, between August and May, and with school an hour's drive down from the forest on a good day, Irina takes her lessons at home. But she dreams of leaving behind the sting of minus 43 degrees, with added wind burn and frozen lashes, for a life in California ... or Tuscany. Anywhere she can wear pretty, floaty clothes and feel her skin tingle in the sun.

Irina remembers what her Babushka told her just before she died, 'Dream as if you'll live forever, live as if you'll die today.' She holds on to that thought every time she opens a glossy magazine and sees shoes. She has a thing for shoes and stands in front of her mirror balanced with her heels on a stack of books, mimicking the trendy baby giraffe pose, dreaming of how it would feel to see her long legs in Christian Louboutins. But then, when she goes out into the forest with her father on a bright, clear, sunny day dressed in her reindeer skin boots and wolverine pelt parka she's humbled to come across a family of grazing musk deer, or witness wolf cubs playing in a snow drift, or cranes soaring over the tree canopy. All taking her breath away. She wants it all.

She has an itch, and it needs scratching.

It's still dark as she trudges out of the forest towards the Vilyuisky Trakt. Through the thinning treeline she sees the twinkling lights of Uncle Igor's truck as it sits waiting. He is taking her and her cousin Alexei on the six-hour drive into Yakutsk and then across the frozen Lena River, where they will continue their journey by train to Chita City. The Trakt is the only link between communities through the vast swathes of forest. The red clay road runs in a straight line for miles down into the Lena valley. It takes all day. The wheels of the truck have no option but to follow the deep rigid grooves of the road, created following one particularly mild, wet summer but frozen solid now. The rising sun fires the red clay, and it shimmers like a never-ending counter of dried, smoked omul at a Baikal fish market.

Shopping for shoes in Siberia isn't like popping into a local town while the washing is on. Irina has never travelled so far from home before, but Alexei is older and has even been to Moscow; he will keep her safe. Uncle Igor drives them the extra 15.6km from Yakutsk to the railway station at Nizhny Bestyakh on the other side of the Lena River. The sun is fully awake now and the light is dazzling. The blue-white ice road has been ploughed smooth, like a pallet knife drawn across a gigantic and frosted Christmas cake, edged with a ribbon frill of green firs. Jumping down from the truck, they watch as Uncle Igor turns the truck around and heads back across the river. He will probably drive all night to get home. Being a single-track line, the train runs south on odd numbered days, and north on the even ones, with none at all on the 31st of the month. Today is the 29th so if it's delayed, they might have to wait three days for a train. Alexei has booked the tickets online which is just as well because the ticket office isn't manned, and the broken split-flap information board has created a whole new language of its own.

Swaddled in their furry fat suits, they shuffle around the station waiting room like a couple of waddling bedrolls trying to keep warm, but it isn't long before there is an eruption of noise, when the train steams into the station in a black stink, oozing oil. The doors clang, the train jolts and hisses, and Irina and Alexei climb awkwardly up the steps into the blue Permafrost Express. Irina is surprised to see how crowded it is on board. Maybe more mad shoppers, hungry for the latest must-haves seen on TV.

It's a two-day ride, but Irina tries not to let the warmth and the hubbub of the carriage induce sleep too soon. She wants to feel and see everything - outside and inside. The taiga forest thins out and they pass through a landscape that flattens to meadows the nearer they get to Skovorodino where they transfer to the grand Trans-Siberian Express for the final leg to Chita. As the sky grows dark again and the windows merely reflect the inside of the carriage, Irina finally sleeps.

The night hours race with the miles to morning and in no time, they're in the big city. Irina and Alexei disembark, hearing welcomes all around them from the greeting of other passengers, and goodbyes from the Provodnista on the train. Irina has never seen so many people. She and Alexei are swept along the platform in a great sea of bodies which pinches and slows as they reach the gate, popping and exploding in all directions once through the other side – onwards to who knows where.

Alexei leaves Irina at the large department store just outside the station and goes off on his own errand, promising to be back to collect her in an hour. They are booked on the early evening train to make the same journey home in the opposite direction.

Irina wastes no time. She's hungry for one thing only. The shoe department. Still in her reindeer boots and thick parka she waves off the concierge who asks if she wants to deposit her outer garments in the undressing room. She is overdressed and slightly overheated by the time she reaches the fourth floor, and the assistant seems wary when Irina approaches her knowing precisely what she wants ... in a size 35 please. The assistant thinks she looks like a 42. By the time the woman comes back with a box and turns back the purple tissue paper Irina is peeling off her layers like a matryoshka doll. She sits down on a studded leather bench and offers her feet like Cinderella awaiting the glass slipper. The assistant gently takes her ankle and Irina slips her silky pink toes into the peep-toe high-heeled pumps and watches in awe as the fluorescent laces are wound around her leg in a criss-cross pattern. She stands up slowly and turns slightly to each side getting the measure of her heels on heels and not on books, until she feels confident enough to walk over to the mirror. Balanced with her feet pointed straight out in front of her, she moves one leg further forward and grins into the mirror as the baby giraffe poses back at her.

Ditched

Christine Hogg

I've always been clumsy. If there's an uneven pavement, I'll trip over it. Low hanging branch, I'll walk into it. There's always so much to do, too much to think about and I'm easily distracted.

I once received the same birthday card from four different friends. A young woman lying flat on her face, with the slogan "Even after 12 vodkas, Charlotte maintained her usual poise and elegance." I couldn't really complain. The week before, I'd tripped and fallen head first into the road and almost got run over by a lorry. I'd only had one shandy though, so it wasn't the booze, it was just... me.

My partner, Don, was never sympathetic. He used to laugh at me, or lecture me to be more careful. Like when I burnt my arm on the iron. I was getting his shirt ready for a Saturday night out with his mates and he distracted me by complaining about the dishes. Or that time I nearly cut my finger off when I was trying to fix the window his friend had broken. Not the nurturing type, Don. He said I should have been more careful. He wouldn't take me to the hospital, didn't want blood on his car seats. In the end I was fine. I got a taxi to casualty and the wound only needed a few stitches, nothing serious.

I've always been alright in the end. Mum used to say I was made of elastic. I always bounce back. I thought everyone was like that.

It seems not.

One day Don and I were on a country walk. One of those rare occasions where I'd persuaded him to come with me for a bit of exercise. It was the first sunny day after weeks of rain and on the way back there was a flooded ditch between us and the car park. Don was waiting to see where I'd go. He said I was sure to pick the slippiest route and fall in the mud, so he'd go the other way. I went to the right and got across fine, while he stepped into the water on the left. It didn't look deep and he was wearing wellies, so it should have been okay.

But then I looked over and he was sinking. Up to his knees. Then his waist. He was just sliding down and down with this shocked expression on his face. It was hilarious. For once he'd done the stupid thing, instead of me. So I was doubled over, almost crying with laughter. Instead of helping.

And then he was gone. Just disappeared under the water. Like he'd never even been there.

I think about him sometimes. How the last thing he ever saw was me laughing, an arm's length away from him.

He should have been more careful.

Hard Boiled

Tough people and tough situations
(hard to crack but worth dipping into)

An Unhappy Accident

Christine Hogg

I remember Mrs Dickson was in a foul mood that day.

'Pritchard.' She yelled my name across the office.

I rushed over to stand in front of her desk, as was expected.

'What have you done with the post?' she shouted, even though I was only a foot away. 'The whole region is unable to work.'

I looked at my feet, waiting for her to explain what on earth she was talking about.

'Well?' she screeched.

I looked up to see her glaring at me, red faced. 'The post?' I asked.

'The whole North West region is missing their correspondence. What did you do with it?'

I started to explain that I didn't handle the mail. Not for two years since I'd been transferred to accounts. Anyway, I thought everyone mainly used email now and everything else had been outsourced to-

She cut me off. I couldn't process her words for the yelling. How do you suggest to your boss that she's forgotten what your job is? I knew reasoning with her wouldn't get me anywhere. It never did. So, I just bit my lip and apologised. 'Sorry Mrs Dickson. I'll go check.' I rushed out of the office.

'Stop running,' she yelled behind me.

When I finally escaped into the corridor, I let the glass door close behind me and leaned on the wall at the side - out of sight. I blinked back tears and tried to calm myself down. How could she speak to me like that, in front of everyone? And why did I keep putting up with it? It was getting worse every week. I really wanted to tell her to stuff her job up her twin-set jumper.

Bill, the Admin Manager, was no wiser than me.

'Mrs Dickson outsourced mail services last year,' he said. 'Let me check with them.'

While he was doing that, I looked up a number for the Carlisle office reception.

'No problem with the post as far I know,' the receptionist said, 'but no-one can work anyway because of the network outage.'

'Network outage?'

'Yes, all the systems are down, email, customer accounts, across the whole region apparently. I understand IT are working on a fix...'

I walked back to the main office. I must have stood outside the door for a few minutes, trying to figure out what I was going to say. Then I pulled hard on the door handle. It was a big heavy glass door, so you had to give it a bit of a yank.

The next thing I knew, Mrs Dickson was hurtling towards me. She must have been opening the door at the same time. She landed sprawling on the carpet near my feet.

She was struggling to get onto her knees. I reached out to help, but she screamed. 'Take your hands off me.'

I jumped back, so that must have been when the trolley got knocked over.

Brenda was bringing refreshments for the eleven o'clock meeting and she can't have seen me. Everything went flying: cups, saucers, biscuits and the huge brown coffee urn that Mrs Dickson always liked to use, even though Brenda could barely lift it on her own when it was full.

I must have been trying to catch the coffee urn as everything tipped over. Instinct I guess. But unfortunately it got swiped right into Mrs Dickson's upturned face.

So that's what I told HR.

Such a tragedy, one of those million-to-one unhappy accidents.

Investigator Required

Susan O'Neal

Calvin shifted position slightly and the mud sucked wetly at his boots. He had been standing in the field for nearly two hours, hidden in the narrow stand of trees, watching and waiting. His arms ached from holding the camera with its long lens, as he checked for any movement from the farmhouse. The windows were closed with the curtains drawn and he hadn't seen so much as a glimmer of light from the place since he'd arrived. The countryside was wide awake now, and a cockerel had been bellowing its reveille since the light began creeping over the horizon. Got on his nerves, that raucous crowing. He'd strangle the wretched thing if he got hold of it. Several cows at the fence were moaning as well. They'd gathered at the sturdy gate, presumably drawn by habit. The soil, churned up into thick collops of sticky mud, was interspersed with the gleam of oily water. Above the mess, the cows' distended udders swung, their fat purple teats silhouetted in the low angle of the morning sun. Surely someone would appear soon, to bring them in for milking? Calvin lowered the camera and rubbed his back. He felt his age today. He was getting too old for this kind of malarkey.

The client alleged visitors to the dilapidated farmhouse had disappeared. Lots of them. He was looking for concrete evidence before going to the police. Sounded a bit farfetched to Calvin. Smelled a funny colour, as his old mum used to say. But the fee for this investigation was tempting. Plus expenses.

Somewhere a dog barked and then yelped. Calvin strained his ears to try and make out what had stopped the dog but he couldn't hear anything above the cows' restless mooing. He should get closer to the place, try and see in. Slipping the camera into the case slung around his neck he started to turn, to get out of the spinney.

'Not so fast,' came a hoarse whisper. 'You stay where you are.'

Calvin froze, as something small and hard touched his back, just above his belt. Ridiculously, he thought it was the muzzle of a gun. Been watching too much James Bond.

'Now look here-' he began.

'Which part of "stay where you are" did ye not understand?' said the voice, accompanied by a non-too gentle poke in his back.

It was an accented voice, with a burr in its hoarseness. An older man? Without looking, Calvin had no idea of the size or age of the man who had come up behind him so silently.

'What do you want?' said Calvin.

'I want you to stand still while I work out what the hell you're doing on my land, watching my house.' The possessive pronouns were spat out - the message was clear.

'I can explain,' began Calvin. 'I was-'

'Shut it.' Another hard poke was very persuasive. Calvin shut it.

It started to rain. Slowly at first, a light pitter patter hit the leaves but it quickly became a downpour and the trees provided no shelter. He shifted his weight, squelching in the sludge and wishing he was anywhere but here. Behind him, the man was patting down Calvin's pockets. Whatever he was looking for, he didn't find it and he yanked Calvin's arm to turn him round, pushing a large handgun into his oilskin pocket as he did so. He was a huge man, his face mostly hidden behind bushy eyebrows and a shaggy brindle beard.

'Who sent you?' The venom in his voice was unmistakable.

Calvin was miserably aware that he was on dodgy ground, probably trespassing and definitely at a disadvantage against this angry giant. He had to be careful.

'I'm doing a survey-'

'Ye're bein' paid to snoop?'

Calvin was reaching into his sodden jacket but caught the man's movement and stopped, his hands held high in front of him. The gun was out again now and being waved about.

'I was just going to show you my ID,' he explained hastily.

'You keep your hands where I can see them.'

'Look, there's no need for that, I'm sure we can sort this out-'

'I'll be the one doin' any sorting. For a start, ye can explain to me why you need that.' He pointed to the camera.

'As I said, I'm doing a survey of the area, getting shots of interesting property and-'

The man cut him off with a snort. 'Yeah, right, you've said that twice over. As you're so keen to look at the house, we'll talk about it inside, out of the rain.'

An invitation into the farmhouse was better than Calvin could have hoped. He nodded enthusiastically.

'OK, lead the way.'

'You go first. And keep your hands up. Don't make me tell you twice.'

Calvin wasn't arguing - that gun unnerved him.

They trudged in single file through the mud, serenaded by the cows. At the door, the man gestured Calvin should go first. Inside, there was a thrumming vibration, beating everywhere in the gloomy space.

The man kicked the door shut behind them, stepped out of his boots and shucked off his oilskin, dropping it on the bare floorboards. Calvin would have liked to do the same. The rain had seeped through his coat and soaked his shirt but as he lowered his hands, the man gestured with the gun towards the stairs at the back of the room.

'Down.'

Clumsily, hampered by his muddy boots on the rickety treads, Calvin went down. There was a rough door at the bottom. Through substantial gaps in the planking he could see small points of mauve light, pulsing and fading, reflected in a small window on the other side of the room. Why hadn't he been able to see that from outside? The vibration was much stronger here, a rhythmic juddering driving through the soles of his feet into his very bones.

'What's in there?' His voice came out as a croak.

'You're the one surveying interesting property. Take a look.'

An ungentle shove propelled Calvin through the door. Across the threshold he stopped abruptly, appalled. Immediately in front of him, the lights were flicking at the roiling edges of a void in the floor, so deep he couldn't see the bottom. Instinctively he slid sideways and pressed his back hard into the wall. He scrabbled either side of his body but there was nothing to hold on to. The shifting dark hole was mesmerising, alive and trying to draw him in.

'What's that?'

'That, my friend, is the future. The solution to overpopulation and the ruin of this planet by leaders who do not care and will not change. We tried a pandemic cull but it didn't deliver anything like enough numbers. Once we've perfected this technique, it'll be the answer.'

'Wha-what is it?'

'This is the first of fifty portals to Mars.'

Calvin could feel the sweat beading on his face, as he struggled to make sense of the words.

'How-how does it work?'

'Why don't you investigate? Do a survey.'

There was no room to manoeuvre. The man reached across and grabbed Calvin's coat. Tugged hard.

Arms windmilling wildly, Calvin overbalanced and fell forward.

Jewels

Christine Hogg

In the five weeks since I joined Haven South, I've developed a habit of waking early and savouring the quiet calm that will soon disintegrate into the chatter of a hundred waking women. Closing my eyes, I imagine that I'm at home, in the times before. Ignoring the rough blankets and constant cold, I fill my head with memories. A soft down quilt; a hot shower with rose-scented bodywash -

'Hey, Mel. You awake?'

I'm jolted from my daydream by Pauline whispering at me from the next bed. I keep my eyes closed.

'Mel... Melanie'

'Shhh,' I hiss, nervous that she'll attract the attention of the Monitors.

'I only want to ask about –'

I shake my head.

'I was only asking,' she grumbles. 'Pardon me for –'

I reach across the gap between our beds and pull myself over so my mouth is next to her startled face.

'Rule three,' I whisper. 'No talking before lights-on.'

'But I only –'

I slide back to my own bed and pull the blanket over my head, turning away from her. If she wants to risk being returned to the outside, she can do that on her own.

When Pauline arrived last night, I'd been thrilled to see a familiar face. None of my real friends or family had made it into the Haven yet. I'd rushed towards her, offering help, suggesting she take the empty bed next to mine in the 3rd women's dormitory. What on earth was I thinking?

In my joy at seeing someone I knew, I'd completely forgotten why I distanced myself from her on the outside. How she tried to recruit every last one of our friends to the 'business opportunity of a lifetime.'

* * *

I'd upset her the very first time she mentioned her new business.

'You sound just like one of those MLM pyramid scheme people,' I'd joked and all the girls laughed.

It quickly became less funny. Every shopping trip, lunch or night out tainted by Pauline espousing the virtues of the gaudiest jewellery we'd ever seen. Ugly twisted plastic and fake gold necklaces, brooches, bracelets, even shoe buckles. Pauline's personality disappeared under the ever increasing weight of trinkets that swamped her petite frame.

She became obsessed with trying to sign us up, demanding we quit our jobs to help her rise through the ranks from emerging emerald to soaring sapphire and ultimately diamond sparkle-knickers - or whatever it was - where she would apparently get a free car.

Eventually we banned the subject of jewellery and Pauline drifted away from our group, preferring to use her social time searching for more willing targets.

* * *

When the lights-on bell begins it's a gentle hum, increasing relentlessly until it reaches fire-alarm level, when the noise suddenly stops and the lights come on. I peek over at Pauline, surprised to see that her face is tear-streaked.

Perhaps recent events have softened her. Heaven knows it's changed all of us. It started with food and water shortages, warnings to stay indoors. We thought it was all temporary, freak weather and supply chain issues that would sort themselves out, just like they always did. But it just got worse and the riots started. Then every day became about survival, finding things to barter or steal, trying to avoid the violence, losing touch with loved ones and not knowing who to trust.

I reach out a hand and pat Pauline's arm. 'I'll tell you all about the rules and routines over breakfast.'

I explain that the Monitors watch everything. Constant vigilance for any sign of unrest that could destabilise the Haven. We'd all seen what happened on the outside, how people could go from civilised to feral in a matter of days. So, anyone who might risk the fragile stability is ejected, making space for one of thousands desperate for a place.

Each day we work for our assigned teams. I'm allocated to the "Sustain" group, with a sub-specialty of Agriculture. I use my scientific background to explore ways of maximising food production in the hydroponic labs.

After breakfast, I show Pauline to the induction area and wish her luck. She is quiet, adjusting to the new environment.

My day in the lab starts with excitement. There is a breakthrough in mineral balance that might increase food production. The whole team is assigned to work out implementation details.

I see Pauline briefly at lunchtime. She bounces along the corridor towards me, her face flushed.

'I've been assigned to Entertainment,' she beams.

I grin back, relieved she's happy with her allocation. "Entertain" is a new group, introduced because people were becoming lethargic, stifled by the rules and routine. I've heard that it's all about competitive sports, there's no time for frivolity in the Haven. The monitors have calculated the most efficient ways of increasing adrenaline for spectators, as well as participants.

'What specialism?' I ask.

'That's what's so great,' she gushes, 'it's jewellery, all my experience is going to be –'

'Jewellery? I don't recall seeing –'

'Jewellery, Jewels, whatever it is. The initiation monitor tried to put me off. Apparently all the other specialists are men, which I don't see as too much of a problem...' She offers an exaggerated wink that makes me shudder. 'I explained that I'm an expert and insisted they sign me up.'

'But,' I'm baffled. 'Isn't entertainment all about sports? Boxing, judo –'

'It's a new specialism,' Pauline explains. 'Super competitive they said, but I'm not worried about that. I'm sure I'll be top salesperson within a week. Must dash.'

'Salesperson?' I watch her bounce off down the corridor.

When I finally finish in the lab and return to the dormitory, Pauline is lying awkwardly on her bed. In the dim evening light I can't quite make out what's wrong. As I get closer, I realise both arms are bandaged and her face is bruised.

'Pauline. What on earth happened?'

She groans, tears running down her swollen cheeks.

'It's not jewellery,' she sobs, 'they lied... it's fighting... it's all just fighting.'

'Oh,' I gasp, light dawning. 'You've signed yourself up for Duels.'

The Rules of the Game

Susan O'Neal

Waiting to buy her train ticket, the tall elderly woman wears her red hat at a jaunty angle over one eye. Her years are beginning to bend her tweed-covered back a little but the gleam in the visible eye belies her age. This one is a duchess, forthright, expecting to be taken seriously, used to having her own way in all things, I judge. Not her, then. The next in line is perfect. Androgynous in jeans with a cropped hairstyle and Doc Marten boots, no eye contact, cool and remote. I nudge Dino. Her. That one. We're playing 'charm school', a favourite game while we're waiting for our train home.

It requires fine judgement, exceptional timing, and the right body language. Many a time we'd had to leg it when someone thought we were about to mug them. Dino got punched in the eye once. Most often we're ignored, two young guys just like the ones pleading for small change shuffling through the train at 11.30 on a Friday night, too drunk to realise the effect they're having. The trick is to transmit I'm no threat while catching the subject's interest and separating them from the crowd, because you don't want some interfering busybody elbowing into the conversation and spoiling everything. The rules are - you have ten minutes to get the subject to give you a fiver, with no threats and no physical contact. We're not in it for the gain, just the glory. You win extra points if they offer more than the fiver, or you get a smile. Double points if they want to stay in touch. It's harder than you might think.

The girl has moved away from the ticket counter and is wandering towards the exit, talking to someone on her phone. She nods twice, abruptly, and finishes the call, stuffing the phone into her jeans back pocket. The other pocket has the outline of a pack of cigarettes. Dino moves in.

'Hi,' he smiles, waving a slightly bent white cylinder. 'Got a light?'

She stops. Gives him what I can only call a sneer.

'Not in here, mate, don't be daft.' She indicates the round No Smoking signs up and down the walkway.

'I'd sell my soul for a fag. I'm gasping.' He makes his funny face - head down, he peers up through his floppy fringe with a lopsided grin, widening his eyes.

'Worst impression of Bambi I've ever seen,' she snorts. 'That supposed to persuade me, is it?'

'I thought it might. OK, if not a light, could you lend me a fiver?' In for the kill, sometimes the direct approach works. He waits, smiling.

'What d'you want a fiver for?' He's only done it. I'm impressed. Once your target engages with you, you're almost there. I see him turn and fall in beside her as she sets off again. She has her lighter in her hand.

'It's like this - I'm on my way to Watford and the dog...'

I groan quietly. The old 'the dog ate my last tenner' again. Well, up to him. I shrug my shoulders to bring my coat collar round my ears and lean against a pillar to wait till he comes back. After a while I get cramp in my calf and have to stamp about a bit. Returning to my pillar, I can't see Dino or the girl so I nip up the iron steps to the second level - you can see the whole station from there. Trains wait impatiently as family groups hurry to find their seats and one or two heavily-laden young travellers, lugging backpacks nearly as large as themselves, bump their way along. The occasional impenetrable announcement from the tannoy increases the confusion as folk hesitate, trying to interpret the jumble of language. Sudden shrill whistles add to the panic - Dino and me reckon they do it for a laugh, to get the rest of us going.

There are refreshment stalls around the concourse, but not the kind you go into, so I can't imagine where they've gone. I go back downstairs. I wish he'd hurry up, there aren't many direct trains on a Sunday afternoon and I don't fancy the stopping one, takes ages to get to our place.

The back of my neck prickles, the way it does when someone's watching you. I turn my head to check, and near the cash machine a flash of colour catches my attention. A red hat bobs round behind the destination board, moving faster than you might expect from a septuagenarian. Still no sign of Dino and the girl. He's had plenty of time to smoke that cigarette and chat her up. Where's he got to? I wander across the concourse looking everywhere, even peering behind the destination display. The woman with the red hat is there, holding Doc Martens Girl in a vice-like grip. The girl is frowning. They're whispering, heads together, but their conversation is so intense, some of it carries over to me.

'I only did it for a laugh.'

'Doesn't matter. He has no idea who you are.'

'That's the whole point, sister. Trick people into choices they wouldn't normally make.'

'Well, I'm here from Compliance. He has rights. Should know who he's dealing with. Rerun that conversation with him knowing the full details, see what happens.'

'You're kidding me?'

'No. Rules are rules. If you want the glory of the hit, you have to do it right. I will report the infringement unless you fix it. And you know what that means...' Red Hat has a nasty look on her face - I wouldn't have argued with her.

'Yeah, yeah. Give me half an hour.'

'You have ten minutes. Starting now.'

I'm thinking this is just weird and where the hell is Dino, when he comes tearing round the corner, red-faced and breathing like a grampus.

'Run. C'mon. Quick.' He grabs me by the elbow and drags me pell-mell out of the station and down the hill towards the big garage at the bottom.

'In here, quick,' he pants, pulling me after him into the shop part.

'What's up? What happened?' I'm breathing hard too, Dino set a cracking pace.

'Gimme a minute.' He's bent forward, hands on his thighs, trying to get his breath back. 'Can you see her?'

'Who?'

'That girl.'

I peer out, between the glossy magazines and the cellophaned flowers.

'Can't see anyone. What's going on?'

'She said, she said - oh god. You have no idea...' Dino is still gasping for air. He wipes away the sweat running down the sides of his face with his sleeve.

'What? Spit it out man, what happened?'

'We were getting on well, she offered me a fiver and a pen. She said "Put your name on it and you can have it." And then, her eyes went kinda funny, glowing and she growled at me "Everything has a price. I gave you a light, I want your soul."'

'What? She was joking - '

'No. You should've been there. I couldn't look away. She paralysed me somehow. It freaked me out.'

'What'ya do?'

'I couldn't do anything. But then that woman with the red hat came by and dragged her away. So I legged it.'

'I think you might be in luck,' I said. 'Did you take the fiver?'

'No.'

'Then you just need to keep out of her way for the next ten minutes. She has rules too. Let me explain...'

Blood Ties

Alison Drury

Kedua stepped off the maglev, one of the few remaining floating trains still working. The outside air felt viscous and Kedua cursed and swatted at tiny yellow-fly which left vivid orange splatters on her sweaty skin. She longed for rain to flush the bugs away. She could have quite happily gone around the loop again to savour the blissful aircon, or maybe to avoid the reason she was here; terrified what the test results might show as the reason for her crushing headaches.

Inside the cool Med Centre, she felt worse; her head pounded so loudly she wondered nobody else could hear it. Her hands shook as she keyed in for her appointment and she jumped as a synthetic voice echoed around the quiet and empty room. 'Good morning. My name is Fai, please go to pod... three... for... Dr Thorsen. Thank you, have a nice day.'

Kedua sat fantasising how many front-desk AI drones had the same name when Dr Thorsen appeared.

'Hello Kedua, thank you for coming in again today, how've you been?' Dr Thorsen ushered her in and indicated for her to sit down.

'OK I guess...the headaches are becoming a real pain,' Kedua winced at her own witticism.

Dr Thorsen sat back in her chair and tapped the tablet on her knee to refresh the screen. 'Your results are back. I have to say, I've never seen anything like it before.'

Kedua sucked in a stuttering breath. Oh God, I've got a brain tumour. Her heart hammered. She tried to mask her anxiety with a weak smile as the doctor looked up.

'Your case is incredible. It's showing a couple of things actually. Firstly, your condition has been identified as Sensory Duplexia...or Triplexia – depending on how many of you there are.'

Kedua looked puzzled, 'What's that?'

'Well, as you know, you're a Multiple from G1? Your mother must have had more than one baby?'

Kedua's mind drifted to the images in her head that felt like real memories; her as a child with a mum and dad, and then older, with a sister – she'd always wanted a sister to share secrets and giggles. She saw her mother; petite but strong, with dark-bronze hair and green eyes – a grown-up version of herself. She longed for a family like that.

'Kedua?' Dr Thorsen was speaking again. 'Do you know anything about your birth parents?'

Kedua shook away her inner thoughts. 'Well, at the Home we weren't told anything much. I suppose we didn't know any different, just thought we weren't wanted. It was only when I left I thought I'd try and find them.' Curiosity had festered long enough, leaving a port wine stain on her heart. She had to know, even if her parents didn't want her. Kedua knew the Gliese Colony Directorate had laid down strict guidelines to avoid the monumental errors that had led to Earth being abandoned. One of these was to control procreation - in order to maintain a manageable population on G1, all families were restricted to one child. The rule applied to everyone and she shuddered. Imagine that. How awful. Her heart ached at the thought of a mother having to give up one of her babies.

'I've looked at the Registry and it seems I was definitely born on G1, but I need to do some more digging.' She didn't elaborate that she was planning to hack into the restricted area to get what she needed.

The doctor nodded. 'That's great. Well done. Anyway, I was talking about the possible reason for your headaches. Let me explain. Sensory Duplexia is when you share all the pain and symptoms from the illness of your sibling.'

'Is that a real thing? You mean I'm not actually sick?' A pressure lifted but the relief was instantly cauterised by guilt. 'But my brother or sister might be?'

The doctor nodded. 'There's something else too.' She hesitated and Kedua wondered what was coming next.

'You've a very rare blood type.'

Kedua leant forward, 'Is that bad? Am I ill?'

'No, no, you're quite healthy...apart from the headaches.' She smiled reassuringly. 'Your blood is Rh-null, often called Golden Blood. It's incredibly rare.' She stood up and came around to perch on the edge of the desk, taking Kedua's agitated hands in hers. 'I'm more concerned about your welfare. I wish now I'd not rushed into logging your report.' She looked rueful, and gently squeezed Kedua's hand, 'I'd like to help you if I can.'

Kedua sharply drew her hands back. 'Whah...what do you mean?' her voice constricted.

'Kedua, this is very serious, for you and your sibling. Golden Blood is universal, it can be given to anyone, including others with rare blood types,' Dr Thorsen dropped her voice, 'and, there's talk of synthesising Rh-null for improving the humanoids – it'll mean there's virtually no chance of rejection.'

Kedua felt fear sliding through her veins like ice, 'I see. You mean they'll want our blood?'

'Precisely. You could become very precious to the GCD,' Dr Thorsen lowered her voice even more. 'Once the humanoids are perfected they'll become the service colony. Future Multiples from G1, like yourself, will be terminated at birth. And what will become of you? You might become a lab rat.'

Kedua had gone home with her head spinning. Then the storm came, bringing with it a deluge of foreboding.

* * *

Kedua had lain awake all that night listening to the electric storm as it crashed and thumped, trying to escape the Vogt Valley. The ting ting ting of the rain, drumming on her container roof, escalated the pain in her head to a higher level. Dragging herself off the narrow bunk she crawled across the bare floor to open the door and sat on the top step. Some of the sound, at least, escaped into the humid air. She leant back against the cold metal doorjamb and watched the water dotting her dusty toes. She sighed as her headache eased a little. The shuttle terminal and service zones were up on elevated terrain, but the surrounding ring of mountains meant it stayed dark till way past sunrise. Today, with the low cloud bringing the unexpected rainstorm, it would be dull all day.

Her home was the last on row twelve of 'B' section. The containers stood on copper-clad staddle stones, to keep out blue sand snakes and terrabeetles, but they also protected it from the flooding. Kedua tried to remember how long it had been since it last rained. Water coursed down the corrugated steel panels, arteries carrying rust-red water into large barrels at each corner of the container. She watched the raindrops bounce high off the hard, dry soil in mesmerising synchronicity until the ground became a dimpled sea.

Life here on G2 was okay – she didn't know any different - but it wasn't great. It was the smallest, and nearest, planet that orbited Gliese 581 and everybody on it supported the larger colony G1. The red dwarf sun was getting hotter and G2 was suffering the most; the glaciers were melting and expanding the oceans, forcing everyone to move to higher ground, crops and livestock were more difficult to raise in the desert-like conditions. Her planet was going the same way that Earth had all those years ago, the reason her ancestors had to seek new habitats.

Kedua thought back to yesterday's conversation with Dr Thorsen and, consumed by a new urgency, decided she must go back to the Registry. Do I have a sister or a brother? Are they sick? Can I help them?

The rain stopped as swiftly as it had started, leaving behind a fresh new fragrance. The yellow-fly and floods disappeared like they'd never been. She wished her headaches would do the same. Over the next week each day after work, she pushed on, trawling through screens and screens of records. Finally, she found what she was looking for. After drilling down through several sub-folders to some half-encrypted data she found lists of multiple births. She hesitated, afraid to read on; for something she'd always wanted to know, she was now worried what she'd find. Taking a deep breath, she ran her finger along the line of her birth date. Bingo, there it is. Three entries, with just one set of birth parents. Pertama, Kedua, and Ketiga. A link took her to scans of their birth registration. For some reason, Ketiga's name had been crossed out and Tiga had been handwritten in red. Kedua swallowed down a sob, had her mother done that? Her imaginary family now had names and they began to feel more tangible. She had family - she just needed to find them. They were unusual names, so it wasn't long before she discovered it was she and Tiga who were here on G2, while Pertama had stayed with their parents on G1.

She couldn't wait to tell Dr Thorsen... and Eduardo.

* * *

In all the years in the Home, Kedua had never met anyone from G1. Her job at the Space Terminal Café had given her no reason to want to change that. She'd inwardly groaned as each pilot swaggered in, full of tall stories and dripping with a 'look-at-me' attitude. A new guy, crisp shirt and shiny boots, crossed the canteen and picked her checkout.

'Hi, I'm Eduardo,' he put out his hand. She ignored it. 'I'm a pilot, just come in from G1.'

No shit. She could tell he was buzzing to tell someone, anyone, about what was probably his first flight down from G1. 'Coffee, Sir?' she asked.

'Um, yes, thanks.' He dropped his hand and looked at her raised eyebrow, 'Oh..., black please, espresso,' he looked blankly at the biometric checkout device she tapped.

'It's not complimentary.' Good lord, he can fly through space but can't navigate a canteen.

He stuttered, and blushed, 'Erm, sorry...like this?' He awkwardly placed his thumb on the reader.

She felt she'd been a bit mean, he seemed different to the others. She chuckled silently as she watched him stick out his tongue in concentration. 'Welcome to G2, this your first time?'

He nodded.

'I'm Kedua, how long are you here for?'

'Just a coupla days this time around, general cargo, but I'm rostered for the bi-monthly Multiple shipments.'

She was a little rattled at his heartless comment.

'Next time I hope to stay a bit longer...perhaps you can show me around?' she heard his confidence growing in his excited chatter.

She placed his espresso onto a tray, 'Oh. How d'you feel about that?'

'What do you mean?'

She could see he was confused. 'Multiples. Shipping unwanted babies?'

'Ahh...,' he paused. 'It's unfortunate I know, but it is the law.'

Kedua sighed, 'Yeah, I know.' More than you realise – you have no idea. 'Have a nice day.'

But gradually, over the weeks, she looked forward to his company and it wasn't long before she was manipulating her shifts to coincide with Eduardo's trips to G2. They shared stories about his family and growing up on the new colony and her life as a Multiple. Several times he mentioned the frequency of her headaches and had seemed relieved when she said she'd get checked out at the Med Centre.

After the diagnosis, when she told him what Dr Thorsen had said, she could see he was worried for her. She'd already told him she was researching her family and, when she discovered Tiga had been sent to a facility on the west coast, she had been very touched when Eduardo had offered to go with her to find him.

Kedua called Dr Thorsen, 'I've found them, I'm a triplet.' She gushed. 'I've a brother here and a sister on G1. I'm going to try and find him first. My friend Eduardo is going to come with me.'

'That's great news,' the doctor said, 'I'll give you a copy of your diagnosis. When you find him, it'll explain everything. Tell him he can call me any time.' The line went quiet for a few seconds. Then, in a more tentative voice, 'Kedua?'

'Yes, I'm here.'

'I don't think you should take the Hyperloop.'

Kedua sensed the doctor might be holding something back.

'I know it'll be quicker, but I'm worried about you being tracked. You need to find your brother as quickly as possible, but you have to stay under the radar, so to speak.'

* * *

The doctor handed Kedua her notes on a DNA data tile and the key to her scratched and dented arterial-red urban rover.

'Not an inconspicuous colour,' Eduardo raised an eyebrow at Dr Thorsen.

'I know, but it'll serve you well, and the spring-mesh tyres means you can take it off-road if you need to. This old model is very reliable, and I still think it's a better option than the Hyperloop.'

Kedua could tell Eduardo was more than eager to drive the old classic, probably very different from the automated controls of a shuttle. She watched as he eased into the cracked leather seat and slid his hands around the worn steering wheel. She almost expected its polished surface to sing like the sound of a wet finger running the rim of a crystal glass. She watched him doing a pre-flight check: adjusting the seat and mirrors to his liking, familiarising himself with the vintage gauges. His tongue brushed his top lip in that familiar tell of concentration.

She laughed.

He looked over, stifling an embarrassed smirk. 'What?'

She shook her head and turned to look out of the window, up into the darkening sky. 'The air was soft, the stars so fine...,' she whispered.

'Jack Kerouac?'

'Wow, you've read On the Road?' she was impressed.

'One of the classics – but Jack looked up at different stars, different galaxy. Buckle up, let's go.'

They set out heading west. The sinking sun forced their shadow to trail longer and longer behind them, before melding with the inky ridge of mountains that hugged the terminal.

The miles slipped by and Kedua felt both nervous and alive, anticipating what they would find at the end of their journey. The night was theirs and the lights shone like lasers down the empty road in front of them. As the landscape changed into open plains, Kedua could see swathes of man-made trees; planted to capture and repurpose carbon dioxide. In the black of night, they looked like regimental rows of ancient war graves. Occasionally, Kedua noticed Eduardo glance in the rear-view mirror, and she wanted to ask what he'd seen. But she didn't, and he never said anything. She felt safe; he was a good driver, the rover sweet in his hands.

After several hours, Kedua stirred as the rover came to a stop. She squinted through shooting white arrows of sunlight as they pierced the flaking tinted windscreen. Stretching like a cat she unfurled her legs from underneath her. The blood whooshed to her dozy muscles, and she suddenly remembered where she was. She sat up abruptly and looked out at what could only be a Surplus Multiple facility. Built to the same spec as the one she'd grown up in; a low granite building with a series of small windows. She wondered whether Tiga had been happy here. Were you lonely too? Did you ever wonder about family?

As they stepped out of the rover, she noticed the air was cooler with a taste of the sea. There was no mountain backdrop and, behind them, the straight road they had just travelled disappeared in a haze of heat. Ahead, the ocean rippled under rows of sentinel wind turbines. Kedua was nervous about the answers that might finally lead to her brother. She didn't think Tiga would still be here, presumably he'd also moved out at sixteen, but hoped he hadn't moved far. The Fai at reception told them to wait for Matron, who wanted to speak to them personally.

The head of the facility was there in moments. 'Hello, Kedua is it?' Matron gave her a saccharine smile and glanced outside. 'Please, come to my office, we can talk there.' She walked past the reception desk, 'Fai, please inform me as soon as my next visitors arrive.'

Kedua instantly felt uncomfortable. She didn't like the woman's tone. She looked at Eduardo and he tightened his lips and imperceptibly shook his head. 'Actually Matron, I think you know why we're here.' Did Dr Thorsen call you, she wondered? 'I may have a brother here, or he was here. His name is Ketiga. Do you know where he might be now?' She didn't miss the second glance Matron gave the main entrance or her slight hesitation before answering.

'Tiga ran away about four years ago now,' Matron frowned. 'He was trouble from the day he came here. Hot-headed. Non-conforming. I suspect he's with the other feral kids that hang out at the old mall. I can't be certain.'

As Kedua and Eduardo made to move away, she hurriedly said, 'Won't you stay, have a drink, you've had a long drive?'

'No, no thank you, we won't keep you.' Something made Kedua feel they needed to leave.

* * *

Eduardo drove slowly through the abandoned vehicles littering the overgrown parking lot of the mall. As they approached the dilapidated entrance, a crowd of youngsters swarmed out of the double doors, surrounding the rover and forcing them to stop. They were like a pack of excited yapping dogs, all different sizes and states of grubbiness. Some ran off back inside shouting and calling one name over and over.

'Tiga, Tiga, Tiga.' Was she hearing right? Are they calling her brother's name?

Eduardo shooed them away to open his door and went to help Kedua out. He steered her towards the shade of the covered main entrance, locking the doors behind them. In seconds there were children clambering all over the rover's running boards, faces pressed up against the darkened windows.

Standing under the rotting canopy, Kedua held her breath and waited. The doors burst open with a crash. Kedua jumped, startled, one hand on her chest and the other on Eduardo's arm. A huge man stepped into the sunlight followed by a dozen or more children who stared wide-eyed at the visitors.

'Tiga?' she inched forward. 'Are you Tiga?' His long, dark-bronze hair was drawn back in a series of braids, and his piercing green eyes were locked onto hers.

'Who wants to know?' he stood with his arms crossed across his massive chest while a small girl ducked out from behind him and hugged his right leg. His demeanour, filthy clothes and pockmarked skin oozed trouble, but he appeared to be the leader of these ragged children.

'My name's Kedua, and this is my friend Eduardo. I...I'm your sister,' she looked up at Tiga for his reaction. 'Your twin - did you know? There's three of us, a sister on G1 as well...with our parents.'

He shrugged.

'We're triplets.'

'And?' He looked down at her but there was something unguarded in his eyes.

This wasn't going well. She hadn't come all this way to be brushed off and Kedua felt her anxiety rising. Tiga was big and scary, but she shook off Eduardo's concerned hand and tried to reason with her brother again.

'We came to find you because I keep getting headaches and the doctor said it might be because I can feel what you feel.'

He started to turn away and she rushed on, 'You might be ill and our blood, we have special blood, rare Golden Blood. Come with us, you're in danger here. If the GCD find you, your life won't be your own. I...'

'Argh, shut up,' he interrupted. 'I'm fine, no headaches. Never needed nobody before... don't need nobody now. Geddit? Said I don't wanna know,' he spat out.

She recoiled like she'd been slapped. 'Here...' Her hand shook as she held out the DNA data tile. 'Take this, in case you change your mind. It's a copy of my notes, and the doctor's number. She can check you over and make sure you're OK.' She looked up at him sadly.

She saw him hesitate before he snatched the tile. 'Special blood, eh? Perhaps I'll sell it to 'em, get rich.' He waved it in the air, 'Thanks.' He turned on his heel and, without so much as a look back, he vanished inside.

Kedua looked down, blinking away stinging tears. She couldn't believe he'd cut her off. The story she'd been playing out in her head for weeks, the one with the happy ending, unexpectedly took a massive left turn, into a very dark place. She felt wretched. Her stomach churned, forcing her to double over, and she almost vomited.

'Come on, leave him. He's an arse.' Eduardo took her arm and gently pulled her towards the rover.

Hardly able to walk and sobbing uncontrollably, she looked up as she saw the children running away.

Eduardo opened the door for her and turned her to face him, 'Listen to me, I think it's the GCD,' he lifted his chin the direction the children had run, '...or their stupid humanoid soldiers. We need to get out of here, fast.'

Over his shoulder, she could see a chrome LanTran slowly approaching, already laden with children, like terrabeetles on an aphid nest.

He pushed her into her seat. 'I'm not sure, but I think they followed us last night. This doesn't look good.' He glanced nervously over the parking lot, hastily pulling her seat belt round her. 'Do that up.'

She froze.

'Now Kedua,' he ordered as he jumped into the driver's seat. 'Let's hope those crazy kids can distract them for long enough so I can get you to the Hyperloop. Then I'll take this, draw them away, OK?'

'What? No, don't leave me. We stick together!'

He started the engine, 'It's the only way. I'll meet you back home as soon as I can, and we can figure out a way to get you on my return flight to G1. Once you're away from this planet you'll be safe – no humanoids up there.'

The commotion with the kids and the shiny military vehicle gave them the opportunity to get away. They took the service road behind the mall heading for the Hyperloop terminal. Keeping to the side streets they drove slowly to remain inconspicuous. At one of the intersections, Eduardo glanced in the rear-view mirror, 'Damn it. We're being followed. Hold tight.'

Kedua looked back and saw a dark truck approaching, flashing its lights. She turned around just as Eduardo accelerated across the junction far too close to oncoming traffic. She hung onto the door handle as he roared off, taking the next left and right, trying to lose their tail.

'Is it them?' he fought to keep the rover straight.

'I don't know,' Kedua twisted to get a better view. 'It's gone, we've lost them.' She let out a sigh of relief.

'Shit! Watch out,' Eduardo slammed on the brakes and their bodies jolted as their seat belts snatched. In front of them, sideways blocking the road, was the truck. 'You OK?'

'What the hell?' she stared ahead, watching Tiga get out of the truck and run towards them.

'Get out,' he yanked open Eduardo's door. 'Gimme the key.'

'Now wait a minute...,' Eduardo started, but Tiga grabbed his arm and pulled him out.

'Shut up.' Tiga shoved him towards his truck as Kedua ran after them. 'Take my truck. I'll take yours.' He watched as Kedua got in the other side. 'Head north for a bit, maybe a day. Then go east. I'll lead them in the other direction.'

Eduardo nodded and signalled for Kedua to buckle up.

Tiga blew out a breath, 'I lied. I do have bad heads... just thought it was normal,' he shrugged. 'I'll call that doctor of yours. Now go. Take it easy.'

She took a last look at her brother, 'And you. I'll find them Tiga. And thanks,' she said.

* * *

Kedua crouched behind the stack of empty transport pods and waited.

Sneaking her on board the return flight to G1 had been tricky, but they'd managed it. 'It'll be uncomfortable, it's a long flight,' Eduardo held her tight and spoke softly against her cheek. 'When you feel the thrusters ignite, everyone will be in their take-off positions on the foredeck. Pop yourself into one of the empty pods.' He pulled back and grinned, 'It's a good job you're so little, it'll be a bit tight - they're built for children.'

The wait gave her time to think. She'd grown up so lonely, crippled by the feeling of abandonment. That's what had initially led her to look for her family but learning about her condition had made finding them crucial.

Eduardo was a great friend but was that enough? She'd see him again. What about Tiga? The raggle-taggle kids seemed to trust him so maybe his tough demeanour was just a front, a cover for his real feelings. Was it the blood ties that had forced his mask to slip? He'd risked so much for her. She had to know.

She slipped off the shuttle.

The Method

Christine Hogg

Professor Margaret Nascence held her breath and and clenched everything. Her fourteen years of teaching experience allowed her to keep the tension hidden from the class.

'Go ahead, Polly. You can do it.' She was careful to maintain the soothing caramel voice tone that swaddled her students in warmth and had them clamouring to be taught by her.

The whole class watched as Polly gulped, rolled up her sleeves and approached the instrument trolley. After a few moments of hesitation she reached out a clumsy hand and grabbed at a silver spiked instrument. Instead of gently cradling the delicate spiculum between two fingers as she'd been taught, the girl grasped it in her large first and raised it in the air like a dagger.

The professor avoided the temptation to duck and considered her options. Polly had seemed the most promising student but perhaps Margaret was losing her touch. She clearly wasn't ready. Other members of the teaching staff would have stopped the girl immediately. Seeing her gritted teeth - and considering what was at stake - any other tutor would take over and carry out The Method themselves, with the reverence it deserved.

The Method:

Light fingers, lighter mind, lightest breath.

Wait.

Listen... feel... connect

Let the new soul choose the moment, then push them through.

This had been drilled into the students for thirty-seven weeks. End to end, step by step, backwards, forwards and endlessly repeated, until they all should have been able to do this blindfolded or half-asleep.

But the training had been under laboratory conditions, with computer sensors. The worst that could go wrong was a less than perfect assessment score and guidance on areas to improve. Performing The Method in the actual ante-theatre, with an actual live subject just beyond the divide, was a whole different matter - as Polly was currently demonstrating. The young student was lurching towards the target with fist still raised and quickly getting closer to the dimensional boundary.

What in heaven did she think she was doing, playing darts? The professor considered her options. Of course accidents happened, and sometimes scheduling was a bit off, not every assignment was expected to be successful. But the first live experiences for new students were proven to have a significant impact on their future success rates. Stopping Polly would keep the students dependent, thinking that they could rely on the professor to save them from their mistakes. Letting her continue to inevitable failure... well, that might traumatise some of the classmates but it would be a quick way to find out which of them could really handle the responsibility of their chosen career.

A gasp from one of the students made Margaret scan their faces. Most looked scared, or even horrified, swinging their gaze from Polly to the Professor, willing her to intervene. Two, Felicia and Patrick, were watching blank-faced, apparently lacking the acuity to understand what was about to happen. Margaret made a mental note to recommend them for management roles, allowing them to graduate with honour, but ensuring they would never be in a position to actually do anything.

She continued to watch as Polly hesitated. The point of the spiculum wavered wildly, millimetres away from the dimensional divide. On the other side, the scarlet-faced human on the bed was screaming as she gave the final push.

The humans naively believed that it was their own clumsy technologies that had increased their success-rates over the years. Bless them. They were completely oblivious to the parallel dimension, where Professor Nascence and her colleagues continued the work of their predecessors, studying the unevolved creatures and painstakingly improving The Method, allowing new life to slip across the divide and meet its target at just the right moment.

Polly stared through the haze into the other dimension. Her fist shook as grim-faced humans worked quickly, calling for a senior registrar and placing a tiny oxygen mask over the face of the pale, silent newborn. Seconds ticked past as machines bleeped, statistics were called out and instructions given by the uniformed team surrounding the tiny human baby.

'Professor... please... help,' gasped one of the younger students.

Margaret nodded. Directly ignoring a student's pleas would look bad in the inevitable report.

'Trust yourself,' Margaret soothed. 'Remember The Method.'

Polly was shuddering, apparently absorbing the pulses of increasing panic that were leaking through the barrier.

Then, from nowhere, Felicia was standing behind Polly and reaching for her raised fist. Felicia closed her eyes and slowed her breathing as she placed her fingers over Polly's and guided her hand. They swayed together and Felicia tilted her head, then gently pushed the instrument through the haze.

On the other side, the still, silent baby began to cry and its pale skin flushed pink.

'Is he okay?' asked the frantic mother. 'Oh, thank you, thank heavens.'

'Thank Felicia,' said the Professor, beaming 'although you'll never know it.'

She grasped the still-swaying Polly by the shoulder and pulled her further back into the room. 'Let's not have you falling through shall we, I think they've had quite enough excitement for today.'

Kevin's Insurance Policy

Susan O'Neal

It took Kevin ages to cut the wood. He understood the principle. You had to put blocks in the bottom of a drawer and then drop in a thin board the exact size to make a false bottom. He'd managed that all right. What he couldn't figure out was how to lift it out again. Which was a pain, as he'd already put his treasures in before he fitted the false bottom. It was such a snug fit that simply inverting it didn't help, the board was stuck solid. He sat back on his heels and wiped the sweat out of his eyes. He had one more thing to hide in his new secret drawer if he could only get into it.

'Look before you leap,' his exasperating mother always said. 'Slow and steady wins the race' was another of her irritating aphorisms. He wished he had paid more attention to this one. He was always in a hurry to get on with things. Sometimes that was good. He'd made many impulse buys on the internet which he really enjoyed. Sometimes, his haste tripped him up. Like now.

He turned to the web as usual. The general advice with secret drawers was to drill a little hole underneath and push a nail in, to dislodge the board. The last thing he needed was a hole in one of his precious things. There had to be another way. And he needed to find it soon, because he had one more item to hide from his mother's prying eyes. It was currently in his jacket pocket, but he needed to put it somewhere more secure.

Kevin had bought the ultimate insurance. A Get Out Of Hell Free certificate. A terrifically nice pastor on the internet had been selling it. It was eye-wateringly expensive but Reverend Simpson assured buyers that it would be worth every penny and there were hundreds of five-star reviews. It came with a bit of a caveat - apparently you couldn't go murdering anyone and terrorism was a no-no, but it would certainly cover day-to-day transgressions. Things like speeding or parking in a disabled spot, for example, or telling lies. With his mother being such a controlling person, Kevin tended to lie a lot. It was the only way he could stop her nagging or giving him the benefit of her continuous advice. Ever since he was little, she had been 'reminding' him to do things.

'Tidy your room,' she nagged. 'Or I'll go in and do it for you.'

It wasn't so bad when he was younger, she never found the drugs. The worst things she discovered were forbidden bubblegum and a lurid magazine, which she inevitably confiscated. Annoying, but he could always replace them from the little shop on the corner. The elderly couple who ran it weren't at all good at spotting shoplifters. These days however, there were several things in his room that he wasn't keen Mother should discover. A chap aged thirty-two tended to accumulate all sorts of items. Some had batteries, one or two of them were silk with lace edgings and then there was his girlfriend. He'd only ever used the inflatable on car journeys. She didn't argue, never wanted to go shopping and was incredibly flexible. While he was waiting to meet Miss Right, she was a very acceptable substitute.

Frustrated with his DIY dilemma, he needed to ask someone for advice. Dave would know what to do. He was the sort of person who could pick a lock, or rehang a door if it got kicked in. Dave wouldn't laugh at him if he saw what was in the cache. He had a few dodgy secrets of his own.

Kevin waited for his mother to leave. She'd done her bothersome best, as she did every Sunday, to persuade him to go to the mid morning church service with her, reminding him that his soul was at risk without regular attendance. It had taken a lot of promising, sincerely, to go next week, to get rid of her. Hearing the door shut behind her, he helped himself to her car keys and manhandled the large drawer with some difficulty onto the back seat of her Fiat 500. She had forbidden him from using it since that unfortunate scrape along the side. It wasn't his fault, the car was just wider than he thought and the bollards unforgiving. This was an emergency and he'd surely be back before she returned. He hurtled left out of their road and shot across the crossroads, overlooking the fact that he didn't have priority. The transporter lorry (which did have priority) hit him side on.

When he came to, he wasn't quite sure what had happened. He was sitting in the road and could see the flattened wreckage of the Fiat under a lorry. He'd have to be particularly creative explaining how that wasn't his fault, since his mother would definitely notice there was more than a scuff along the side.

'OK mate?' inquired a voice beside him. It belonged to a tall youth in a theatrical flowing cape. 'That was a nasty coming-together, you were lucky to get out in one piece.'

He offered his hand and Kevin was glad to grasp it, to pull himself to his feet. He felt a bit shaky but otherwise surprisingly alright.

'Come on then.'

'Come on where?'

'We have to go and see Lucy about accommodation. I'll take you. My name's Damien.'

Kevin found he couldn't resist and fell in beside Damien, hurrying to keep up with the youth's long strides. They turned into an alley and Damien knocked on a huge door, studded with metal. It swung open and the pair stepped into the stygian gloom.

There was a reception desk immediately in front of them framed by a red neon light.

'Lucy, this is Kevin - car crash, ten minutes ago. His fault.'

'Well, not entirely-' began Kevin.

The glamorous redhead interrupted him. 'I think we all know that's a lie. You've precisely three minutes to explain why you shouldn't be cast into the depths of Hell for eternity. Begin.'

Kevin was glad he'd planned ahead for this eventuality. He rummaged in his pocket and produced his precious certificate.

'Here, I think this will help.'

'Oh yes?' She took it and held it by one corner. 'What's this?'

'It's my Get Out Of Hell certificate. I expect you've seen one before?'

'Yes I have, actually,' smiled Lucy. 'But there's a bit of a problem with this one.'

'There is? Reverend Simpson assured me it was the real thing. I paid a lot of-'

'It's a fake.'

'It can't be. He said-'

'I can assure you it's false. The real ones are printed in gold on vellum. This one's red on parchment. It's a cheap copy.' She waved the paper about and it burst into flames. 'Oops.'

Kevin's eyes widened as he watched it burn. He had a long list of transgressions, his get out of hell thing was a fake and he was at the doors of eternal damnation, discussing admission with a redhead called Lucy.

'Can I phone my mother?'

You Should Have Said

Christine Hogg

Jackie ran a hand through her hair and switched off the mute button. 'If I could – '

Her voice was drowned out again by Bill. She waited until he paused for breath then raised her voice a little, 'Can I just say –'

'No need to worry about details now, Jackie. This is just high level scope,' said Bill.

'But, I want to explain that –'

'Are we done here?' asked the CFO.

'We just need your approval for the plan,' smiled Bill, 'all three phases, if you agree.'

'But, it's not –' Jackie started.

'Great. All three phases approved. Good job everyone.' The CFO took a moment to beam sincerely into the camera. 'Now deliver it all. I'm counting on you.'

'But, it's –'

Meeting Ended flashed up on the screen. Jackie slumped over the desk with her head in her hands.

A ping made her look up. Quick Chat, 3:15pm. It was a meeting invite from the head of HR.

Damn, what have I done? Jackie wondered. She checked the clock. 3:07. Just enough time to run to the bathroom and grab something to eat. She was starving and desperate for coffee.

Her laptop pinged again. Another invite from Bill. Project kick off 3:30 – 5:30 pm. She groaned and ran downstairs.

In the living room, Jackie's husband looked up from his phone. 'I told you lunch was ready three hours ago.'

'I'm sorry, Paul. It's been a hell of a day.'

'You can't keep letting them do this to you. You must be allowed a lunch break?'

She stared at the floor. Not trusting herself to speak. Since Paul was made redundant they really needed her income.

'I left yours in the oven,' Paul said. 'On low, but even so, it'll hardly be fit to –'

'It'll be delicious.' She rushed into the kitchen and rescued the dish of – whatever it was.

Paul came up behind her. 'Eat it here. Let's chat.'

'Sorry. I have a –'

'– meeting. I know. When do you not have a meeting?'

'Sorry,' she said again and headed for the hallway.

'Jackie –'

'I can't, I –' she snapped back, then realised he was holding out a mug of steaming coffee. She almost dissolved into tears.

He held up a chocolate bar and gently dropped it into her pocket. 'In case it's any help.'

They smiled sadly at each other for a moment before she rushed back upstairs.

In her office, Jackie took a gulp of coffee and shovelled lunch into her mouth. She chewed furiously at dried up cheese and potato, while typing her password. It was 3:18 pm.

Incorrect Password

Damn. She tried again. Same result. Her heart was racing. She took another gulp of coffee, checked the Caps Lock key was off. Success. She opened Zoom.

'Jackie,' said Olivia, the Head of HR, 'so glad you could make it.' Her jammy red lipstick smile dominated the screen.

After Jackie apologised profusely for her lateness, Olivia got straight to the point.

'It's month five of your probation. Not long until decision-time about whether you'll be offered a permanent role.'

Jackie nodded stiffly, wondering what was coming. She couldn't afford to be out of work again. Not now.

'At your three month review, we set some goals for you. Do you remember?'

'Ermm... yes...' Jackie racked her brains, 'the goals were... about being a team player, making a positive contribution.'

'Exactly.' Another jammy smile. 'How do you think it's going?'

'Ermm... well... it's sometimes tough, with all the meetings, but I'm keeping on top of the work and even solved the –'

'Jackie.' Olivia was shaking her head. 'Of course, the work is important, but you also need soft skills. You're part of a team now.'

Jackie nodded.

'Some... concerns... have been raised. You need to work on appearing more positive in meetings, more supportive.'

'But, if you mean –'

'Jackie. This is exactly the problem. It's very bad form to keep interrupting your colleagues with "But". It's called butting in. Did you know that?'

Jackie stared at the screen biting her lip.

'I've arranged some urgent training for you. Sending it now.'

The invitation arrived in her Inbox.

Jackie almost swore but composed herself. 'I'm very grateful for the training, b-... just, I see it's at 4.30 this afternoon and I have another meeting.'

Olivia shook her head, sadly. 'I understand that you're struggling with time-management and prioritisation. I'm sure we can help.' She clicked her mouse a few times. 'I've arrange a time-skills course for you too. Let me know how you get on.' She ended the call.

Jackie gave up chiselling at her dried-up lunch and pushed it to the side of the desk. She unwrapped the chocolate and pushed chunk after chunk into her mouth, chewing furiously. The project kick-off was about to start.

She heard the front door open and close, then tiny footsteps on the stairs.

'Mu-um, we did drawings at school and I got –'

'Shush darling.' Paul's exaggerated whisper floated up the stairs. 'Mummy's very busy with something very important. Let's go play in the garden.'

Jackie clenched her fists as her calendar beeped. Taking a deep breath, she joined the meeting.

Bill was already in his element, shoulders back and chest puffed out as he pontificated to his Zoom audience about the newly-approved project. He had invited all the regional heads of sales, marketing, operations and finance, most of whom were nodding in agreement.

Jackie stayed muted as she listened to Bill explaining the scope, talking through the presentation that she had created for him.

'Congratulations Bill, fantastic proposition,' someone said, and Bill looked suitably modest as he took full credit for Jackie's work.

As Bill clicked onto the next slide and started talking about phases, Jackie resisted the urge to interrupt. 'Idiot,' she muttered, biting savagely at the last of her chocolate bar.

'Hey Bill.' The soft voice of the North region Sales Director broke in. 'Could I just check something?'

'Sure. Go ahead.'

'You have approval for all three of these... phases?'

'Absolutely,' said Bill proudly. 'We have a full green light from the board and the press release committing to delivery of the whole programme has already been issued.'

Press release? Jackie thought she might hyperventilate. She opened a web browser and did a quick search. It was all over the trade press sites already and even some mainstream media.

'Right...' said the Director. 'Just, it says options on the slide there. Is it options or phases?'

'Oh yes,' another voice joined in, 'I did wonder about that... how is it possible to do one, two and three? They seem... contradictory.'

A lively debate began, with everyone discussing how each phase seemed to undermine the others.

Bill's face grew redder and his eyes widened, blinking at the screen. 'Well,' he said finally. 'This is Jackie's proposal.'

Jackie adopted a neutral expression, aware that all eyes would now be on her.

'Jackie, clarify how all the phases follow on from each other.'

She unclicked the mute button. 'They don't,' she said flatly. 'They are options. We can only do one of them.' She clicked mute again.

'What the f-' Bill exploded. 'You were in the meetings earlier, Jackie. I mean we talked about this for hours. Why the hell didn't you say anything?'

Jackie considered her response. She reached for the lid of her laptop and slammed it closed, cutting off the call, then she popped the final piece of chocolate into her mouth and headed downstairs to her family.

Trapped

Alison Drury

He had been driving for hours and hadn't had a rest stop. He wanted to get home before the game and knew this road like the back of his hand so put his foot down. The sun was already low in the sky and the light flickered intensely through the branches as he passed the edges of the forest. The strobing light was intense and hurt his eyes but as the forest suddenly became denser, his eyes took too long to recover. Fumbling for the light switch, and travelling too fast, he misjudged the first of the bends where the tree line followed the river. The truck slammed through the undergrowth, the brakes having no effect on the steep bank.

Knocked out momentarily, he woke to find the water was seeping in, baffled by the carpet, and rising, now above the pedals. Panicked, his boots sloshed as he frantically tried to release the seatbelt, but it was jammed tight. It was awkward with the steering wheel in the way, but he brought his feet up, as high as his knees would allow, and unlaced his heavy boots, finally kicking them off and throwing them into the passenger footwell; they would just weigh him down more.

He remembered he had some wire-cutters in his tool bag which was on the floor behind the passenger seat. Could he reach it? He pulled his arms free of the seatbelt and, with his legs out straight and ankle-deep in the water, he pushed up as high as he could go and stretched his free arm over the back of the seat towards the bag. Almost, his fingertips tantalisingly close, brushing the canvas bag – but not quite near enough to get a hold.

Time was running out. The water, in just those few minutes, had now risen to his mid-calves and would soon be up to the centre console. Still restricted by his seatbelt, now tight around his hips but with his arms free, he leaned across to the glovebox and managed to flip it open. He vaguely remembered his Mum had left a small umbrella in here; not that he needed it; the water rising up rather than falling down. He pulled out some papers and then saw its familiar shape, sat on top of the first-aid box. As he gently tugged on the corner of the box the umbrella came with it and, as soon as he could reach it, he grabbed it before it fell out into the footwell.

Reaching backwards again, he used the umbrella as an extension to his arm and hooked it into the handle of the tool bag and lifted. It was a dead weight, from both his tools and the water-logged canvas. But he moved it just enough to get a firm handhold and lift it over to the front, relieved he had continued with the weekly sessions at the gym – perhaps boxing would save his life. He gave it a couple of seconds, flexing his fingers to encourage the oxygen back, and then ripped open the bag searching for the cutters.

The engine had stopped but he had the forethought to open all the windows as he knew, once the electrics went, the truck would be totally inescapable. The dying whir of the motor sent the cab black and silent, except for the metal chassis creaking as the truck bobbed deeper and deeper down. With the darkness outside, it wasn't easy to determine where the wet and dry blackness joined. His fingers fumbled. He tried to remain calm as he cut through the belt and, with the water now almost up to the windows, his body was released. He ducked his head through the window and, as the surge of water finally came rushing in, he pushed out and away.

Game still on.

Scrambled

Broken and gently stirred, brought together
into a delicious experience

The Poacher

Alison Drury

It was the height of summer now and a pair of swifts were already fed up with their lodger. He came around late May/ early June; as the sun began to raise its mellow head after the spring rains. He just swooped in. The swifts thought he would be no bother, appearing harmless and quite polite... but a bit of a loner. He was a stocky guy, surprisingly much larger close-up than expected, and sometimes appearing a little gruff and ruffled at the edges. He had unblinking, piercing blue eyes and suffered from a perpetual flaming red boil on the end of a humungous beaky proboscis. He lumbered across the deck, dragging his big leathery feet, and spent hours looking out to sea; his stance erect, his long sleeves clasped behind his back, like a maître d'. He posed importantly with his chest puffed out and a dob of drool dribbled onto his front. His beady eyes scooted and rolled, taking everything in but, all the time, his head remained static, like a Grenadier Guard. He was oblivious... or unbothered... to the south west breeze that lifted his oatmeal coat revealing a dark silver-grey velvety lining.

Water droplets fell and latched on invisibly, like little diamonds carried on the wind. If they rolled, they twinkled with rainbow prisms in both the sun and moonlight.

He waited patiently for hours, occasionally moving to transfer his weight from one foot to the other. In the morning, when the night sky finally turned lilac as the sun loomed above the buildings in the harbour, or in the evening when the sun slipped, like runny honey, into the sea at the end of the day, his alter ego emerged – like someone had flicked a switch. Something in the air caused him to become agitated and he began an incessant cacophony of banging and scratching and screaming and caw cawing. He stamped his feet and threw his head up and down and anybody nearby shrank back and looked the other way, avoiding eye contact with the weirdo.

Every day was the same. The swifts would flit about all day long, doing chores and keeping tabs on their little family. When they came down to the boardwalk, one or the other would invariably have to dart back out to check on the babies, but they would swiftly fly back, skilfully skirting around and ignoring his hangry display.

All the while, the crashing waves rolled backwards and forwards, leaving a popping froth around the granite that grew out of the sea foam. Life for the residents was busier and more abundant when the tide was in and so, as the water gradually abated, they inhaled the salty sea air and settled themselves down in their usual place for a few hours respite before the tide turned again. They watched as the black rocks revealed their jaunty, striated and angular shapes; all leaning back in the same direction like sailors hauling in something huge, as yet unseen, from the sea.

After a strenuous day of foraging in the deep water the warm breath of the sun licked their caps and blow-dried the pebbles under the deck... and then he came crashing in. Like a robust and clumsy toddler. He stood balancing atop the rocky outcrop just off to the side of the deck earnestly surveying the rolling water. He appeared to be waiting for something – for several hours sometimes – before moving off up along the beach. There was peace for a while, but he was soon back to stake his claim on his favourite perch, sounding off to anyone who cared to listen.

At every low tide a small blue and white boat, with a popping outboard motor, chugged out of the harbour. A man in dark green oilskin waders, held up by fraying yellow braces, sat low in the back of the boat using the tiller to guide him to the red buoy bobbing a few hundred yards offshore. Smoke from his pipe billowed out behind him, latching on and winding into the smoke from the engine, leaving a bluey-grey ribbon bouncing just above the water. The poacher was always back on his rock by then, ready and waiting, following this scene intently. The fisherman slowed the engine, and he left the tiller while he reached to haul in the line from under the buoy. Finally, at the end of the line, a dripping basket was lifted into the little boat. The poacher would become more and more agitated; shouting and calling and hopping from foot to foot. When he couldn't contain his excitement any longer, he shot off his post and made his way down across the slippery rocks and over the pools to get nearer – all the time continuing to shriek. They had an unspoken agreement, the poacher and the fisherman, and the contents of the basket were inspected and either dropped into a bucket on board or flung back out into the water, sending the poacher into an absolute frenzy. If he was lucky, he grabbed a titbit, taking it back to the deck and anchoring it down with his feet and tore it to pieces. Satisfied momentarily he stood his ground, glaring daringly in case someone tried to wrestle it off him.

Finally, satiated and with civility returned, he preened and picked at his overcoat, smoothing the creases and adjusting its fall. It was only when the sun melted into the inky water he eventually moved off and peace would return for a few hours – but he would be back at dawn.

This went on for several weeks and then, one day, the red buoy disappeared; the fisherman had moved to a more bountiful crab and lobster garden much further away from the shoreline. Peace returned to the boardwalk as the poacher left his post and forlornly wandered up and down the damp ribbon of sand, his feet leaving heavy heart prints in ever-widening rows along the strand.

And then, one particularly quiet evening, a familiar muffled sound could be heard over the gentle lapping of the tide. The poacher dozed lethargically at the far end of the beach, his tummy rumbling in time to the chugging of the little blue and white boat as it emerged from around the headland aiming for the beach, heavily laden and low in the water. Brimming with lobster pots full to bursting, the fisherman brought the little boat in as far as he could before jumping out and hauling it across the sand and seaweed. The poacher couldn't run fast enough, and half flew, low across the shingle, to meet his friend. The fisherman laughed as he watched the poacher bouncing up and down for joy in expectation, doing a dosey-doe dance between the boat and the baskets. Thrilled that his supper was almost served, the poacher began to sing and keow, nodding his head and snapping his beak – the saliva of anticipation strung almost to the ground. The fisherman went to work sorting his catch, putting the largest specimens into restaurant-bound boxes stacked against a trailer, and flinging the rest back into the surf. The poacher was almost apoplectic until finally the fisherman flung a morsel his way. He had to run to snag it, almost tripping over his big feet, as it sailed too far and over the little blue and white boat. At the last moment, a large black shadow eclipsed the remaining evening light, and with a whoosh of beating wings, the catch was snatched away. Incensed, the long-waiting diner keowed 'Thief! Thief'.

Why is a Raven Like a Writing Desk?

Susan O'Neal

'It happened.' She was desperate to make them understand.

'Of course, you believe it did, dear.' The nurse was soothing, patting her hand. The doctor said nothing, marking boxes on the clipboard. Staying neutral.

Ally snatched her hand away.

'Don't patronise me. I know what I saw. I have to get back. Go after him.' She strained forward, to rise from the chair but the nurse held her down.

'Now, my dear, take your time, catch your breath. You've had a bit of a shock. Probably a reaction after you bumped your head and-'

'The rabbit was talking, he was. He checked the time as he rushed past me and then bolted down- '

'Wait, back up a bit- "checked the time" you say?' The doctor raised an eyebrow.

'Yes.' Ally brushed away the interruption with a flick of her hand. 'I said that already. He was enormous, big as me and wearing a coat. He seemed to be in a tearing hurry and nearly knocked me over.'

In the pollarded beech outside, three ravens were perched on a knobbly branch.

'Quit your shoving,' said the smallest one at the end, 'I can't see what's happening.'

There was much shuffling and huffing as the speaker edged closer to the window, gripping the rough bark with hooked feet.

'She's trying to tell them... Not having much luck though.'

'Not surprised. Those medical types think they know it all,' said Rene, straightening an errant flight feather.

'And what would you know about it?' said the largest raven in the middle, with some asperity. Reg was inclined to pomposity on occasion.

'Will you both just shut up and let me listen.' Ronnie turned back to peer through the window, one beady orange eye taking in the scene.

* * *

The doctor had left the room, instructing the nurse to settle Ally into bed and prepare her for some tests. The nurse bustled off, presumably in search of the necessary needles, swabs and test tubes. Her footsteps echoed back along the landing. Ally sank back into the chair, brows furrowed with the effort of considering her options.

'C'mon Ally, this would be a good time to get a move on,' hissed the smallest raven.

Almost as though she had heard, the girl rose and ran from the room, taking the opposite direction from the nurse's steady course. Along the corridor she raced, sweeping around corners, running hard for the hospital exit, her feet slapping the shiny vinyl with every stride. Outside in the warm summer air, she crossed the parking area, turned left into the lane, vaulted over the fence and raced through the field, breathing hard, arms pumping, heading for the woods. Overhead, the three flapping ravens kept pace, calling to each other.

Ally caught her foot in a tussock and fell, sprawling full length. The impact knocked the breath out of her. Her hand-me-down boots were a constant challenge, but her mother said she must be grateful she had any footwear at all, things being as they were. She sat up, untied the long laces and pulled off her boots. She rubbed her twisted ankle. It seemed to change shape even as she looked at it, puffing up and flushing a blotchy red. She sighed with frustration and looked around for help. From this lower perspective, the view was dramatically different. She could see flattened pathways in the tall grasses, all converging on a gap in the hedge fifty metres ahead, shaded by a clump of trees. It looked for all the world like an arched doorway beneath the branches. She tried to stand but when she touched her foot to the ground jolts of pain ran up her leg and made her gasp. She sat down again awkwardly and began to cry, great wet blobs running down her face.

The ravens banked in a graceful curve once they realised Ally had stopped.

'What's she sitting down for?' began Reg, circling. "Doesn't she know we're on a tight schedule here?'

'Don't think it was entirely her choice, she seems to have damaged herself,' said Ronnie.

'So what happens now?' Rene asked.

Gliding on a warm zephyr, they considered the options.

'We'd better go and tell him,' said Ronnie. 'Rene, you stay here to mark the spot and keep an eye on her. Reg and me will nip off for help.'

'Reg and I,' corrected Reg.

'Whatever. Come on.' Both birds turned and flew fast under the shadowy hedge. They reappeared a few moments later, perched on the shoulders of a large white rabbit. The rabbit paused beside the hedge and pulled an enormous watch from his coat pocket. He stared at it and then shook his head crossly. Shoving the timepiece back into his pocket, he set off across the field, his wildly wagging ears almost unseating his passengers who flapped their wings and gripped the tweedy fabric more tightly.

'Over here,' called Rene, circling lower.

'What's all this then?' asked the rabbit, startling Ally, who had her eyes scrunched shut, trying to stem her tears.

'My ankle,' she sniffed. 'I think I've broken it.'

'You should look where you're going, a great big girl like you shouldn't be falling over at your age,' said the rabbit, folding his arms across his chest.

'It wasn't my fault. I was trying to get out of that hospital place. They think I'm hallucinating or something. They want to do tests on me.' She wrinkled her nose, Close to, the aroma of garlic and parsley on the rabbit's breath did not disguise how awful his feet smelled. Ally tried to shuffle backwards as the rabbit leaned in closer, peering at the girl.

'Whose fault was it then?' the rabbit wanted to know.

'Yours of course. You should have waited. And maybe the boots. A bit.'

'Them boots?' he asked ungrammatically, pointing.

Ally looked around in an exaggerated manner. They were the only boots in sight.

'Yes, those boots. My boots.'

He regarded the boots with interest. They were black and the leather was cracked and worn. The soles were coming away from the uppers in a couple of places. Plenty of life left in them, her mother had said. They must have been handsome when they were new but had been through several siblings before Ally got them. She had to tie them tightly to keep them on.

'No wonder you tripped yourself up. They're far too big for you. What was your mother thinking?'

'That's ridiculous,' said Ally. 'You're a rabbit, what would you know about boots? And leave my mother out of it.'

The rabbit hunched his shoulders, dislodging the ravens, who took off and joined Rene in an aerial ballet.

'I know,' he began haughtily, 'that people who wear such ridiculously large boots that they trip themselves up are in no position to comment on rabbits whose sensible feet always keep them upright.'

'Now just a minute-' interrupted Ally.

The rabbit held up a paw to stop her.

'-and I also know that if we don't get a move on, this story will never get going. You're supposed to follow me across the field, through the hedge and down the rabbit hole. Come on, we're behind schedule already.'

He reached down and gripped Ally under her arms, hoisting her up.

'Upsadaisy. Can you walk?'

'I don't think I can.' Ally touched her stockinged foot nervously to the ground.

'Well, you'll have to hop then. Hold on to me. And bring them boots. Come on.'

A Day Trip to Tangier

Alison Drury

I lie still, savouring the breath of jasmine on the breeze as it lifts the cotton from my skin, and watch the sun trickle across the bedroom floor like spilt Prosecco. I love this. I've finally found my little bit of heaven. I smile in anticipation of strong black coffee as Tarik clinks cups and hums to the tinkling of jazz in the kitchen. People might say I've been unlucky, but I disagree. Four years on, I remember how it all began.

* * *

When Marianne suggests Tangier, we can't agree fast enough. Living in southern Spain, the short flight to Barcelona is our farthest day trip so far. Marianne had grown up in Tangier and she promises us knocked-off handbags and a day to remember. I offer to take us over on the yacht, and I smile to think what Brian would have said – we'd need sailing logs and boat shoes – and to behave responsibly.

'Get the ferry, Jessie.' He'd have said. 'Then you can have some fun mingling with the hoi polloi.' Arriving on a yacht, we wouldn't stand a chance with the Moroccan traders; they'd start with even more highly inflated prices than normal, and I do like a bargain.

Little did I know it was a wholly different day to the one I'd bargained for.

* * *

The Tangier ferry is booked for nine o'clock and we meet in Tarifa, at Café 10. I get there far too early – the proclivities of a punctuality pedant. I'm on my second espresso when Marianne walks in.

'Hola Jessie darling,' we hug and kiss a Spanish greeting over the hubbub reverberating around the busy café. 'Is Babs not here yet?'

I shake my head and signal the waitress over, 'another café por favour ... con leche.'

'Gracias Jessie,' Marianne catches the waitress' arm, 'and tostada por favour?'

The humidity, already high, makes me glad I've chosen a long floaty dress today. I envy Marianne's Danish genes, being able to pull off powder-blue tailored trousers in this heat but love her friendship more. The three of us couldn't be more different. Babs hadn't been anywhere until dragged out of London as a British Consulate wife and I'd sailed the world with Brian until he took a Hedge Fund job with Marianne's husband. Even after Brian died, they didn't let me take myself too seriously. When I announced I was turning vegan, I didn't expect them to join me or go out of their way to accommodate my new enthusiasm for plant-based foods. Despite their light-hearted ridicule, it was cheering to know their overriding concern had been can you still drink Prosecco? From then on, my bag always had emergency vegan provisions of kale crisps and granola bars. And vomit sacks. Yep, a sea-sick sailor – go figure.

The waitress sets down Marianne's order which prompts me to check my own food supplies. It's all good, except, oh no. 'Shit.'

'What?'

I look up at Marianne, her tostada mid-forkful. 'I think I've left my passport on the hall table.'

'No! You sure?'

I rummage again amongst the snacks - the day doomed before it'd even begun.

I jump up just as the last of our group comes into the café, 'No worries... Hi Babs... I'll grab a cab, won't be long.' The door bangs shut behind me but not before they hear me shout, 'hold the ferry.'

I run to the taxi rank around the corner, while contorting my arms into my rucksack straps. Perfect, there's a guy astride a big red bike, waiting and available – that'll be quicker.

'Rápido, rápido. Calle Isabel por favour,' I ignore his headshaking as he points to my dress and espadrilles. 'Emergencia, I need my passport, let's go, vamonos,' gesticulating to the spare helmet.

'Okay, crazy lady.' I can just see his eyes roll behind his visor as he hits the starter, and I hitch up my skirt and swing my leg over the back of the bike. He rides off cautiously, at a creeping pace. This won't do, so I poke him in the back, squeeze with my knees and wrap my arms tightly around his waist – he gets the message and bangs the bike down a couple of gears and roars off, away from the port. We make it home quicker than I can retract the roof on the Vanquish, and back to the ferry with two minutes to spare, which earns him a tip and a big grin. I get a cub scout salute and shake of the head; first crisis averted.

But an hour later, whilst trying to complete the immigration form on the choppy Straits, the agitated espressos turn me a bit green. Queuing to disembark, I unwittingly extend both sick bag and passport; the immigration officer chooses the latter. Flipping open each of the three passports, he gives a ceremonious thwack on each with the entry-stamp and waves us towards the gangway like irritating flies.

We join the surprisingly few foot passengers in the taxi queue bound for Tangier Old Town while a stream of vehicles rolls off the ferry. One, a dusty old VW campervan, is laden with bicycles and trunks and has more rust than paint. As it chugs down the ramp I remember my early days island-hopping with Brian – from the freedom of the open seas, to stepping off and becoming immersed in different cultures.

My reverie is interrupted by the low growl of a motorbike riding down the outside of the queuing cars. It comes to a rumbling stop. The rider turns to look directly at me and imperceptibly nods. I can sense the others haven't seen and are already moving towards a taxi, but I'm transfixed. Is this the same guy from earlier? He stares at me far too long; I can't look away. I feel a flicker of interest, my pulse in rhythm with the deep engine vibration; a reminder of feelings long gone ... immediately followed by guilt.

'Come on Jessie, let's go.' Marianne's voice seems to be far away.

He breaks the moment, flipping down his visor, does that gear shift thing and roars off in a spray of spitting gravel. Don't be daft, I almost snort.

Wearing a wry smile, I climb into the taxi, joining Babs on the foldouts behind the driver. It's stifling, the windows are open but, facing backwards, the draught just plasters my hair to my face. I twist and hold it in a ponytail as I watch the white concrete docks melt behind us like flat bergs into the Mediterranean. The main road snakes up and up and splits into the venules of the Kasbah. The buildings morph from chick-pea sandstone to streets of art, overpainted in cool peacock blues and greens. As we arrive in the Moorish old town of the Medina, rugs hang like ornate flags from the balconies, vibrant in spiced tangerine and ochre. Where the road gets too narrow to go any further, the taxi driver stops and hops out to open the doors.

'Thank you, ladies, have a nice day.'

I glance up and down the almost deserted street. Empty barrows and baskets barricade carved cedar doors. The waving rugs and a few tatty shop awnings offer the only shade. A small group of Berber women in stripy aprons huddle on the pavement, grinning toothlessly from beneath their humbug hats. In a doorway, two old men are framed in a haze of tobacco, leaning earnestly over their backgammon board.

'Excuse me, are all the shops closed?' Babs asks.

'Oh yes Madam, I finish now, rest of day off. Is the Big Holiday.'

'The Big Holiday, what's that?' I ask.

'Eid al-Adha festival, three days. Today is second day.'

'Oh God.' Marianne slaps her forehead.

'But we've come specifically for shopping.' Babs says indignantly.

Marianne's face is ashen, 'I completely forgot about that.'

'Is there nothing open at all?' I urge, trying to avert crisis number two.

'No, no shops open – maybe later,' the taxi man shrugs and gets back into his cab.

With dirhams burning holes in our pockets, we set off along the twisting, turning tangle of streets and up and down mosaic tiled steps. We can hear families celebrating in hidden courtyards full of music and laughter. And another sound, a different tune above the music - is it bleating? Around the next corner we pass a young girl leading a sheep on a leash. A smaller child rides on its back, gripping the make-shift collar and, spotting us, wallops the sheep's rump. The trio accelerate away, the children giggling and squealing. As we make our way ever upwards towards the Kasbah there are more sheep at every turn; button black eyes track us, woolly bodies back away straining against ropes tied to lampposts and scooters. My stomach constricts as I battle with the exertion and the woodsmoke which fills the air, laced with roast garlic and warm spices. It gets more surreal by the moment. The turns get tighter and the buildings taller and the shadows longer. Suddenly, out of the blackness of a side-alley, a young man steps out. He's wearing jeans and a dirty white vest under a black leather jacket that's far too big for his scrawny frame. A serpent tattoo winds up from below his collar, pulsing along his neck muscle.

'Pretty ladies, you want some kif, have a good time?' He offers his lit cigarette.

'Oi,' I start, and march up to him. 'Listen, buddy, back off.'

'Careful, Jessie...'Babs implores.

He turns towards me with narrow shifty eyes. 'You very beautiful too. Come, I take you to shop, everything you want.'

'No, we're fine, thank you.' My throat tightens at the rancid hair oil and stale nicotine. Before I can stop him, he yanks my bag from my shoulder and runs off into a dark alleyway.

'Oi,' I shout again. I start to follow him instinctively, but he's ten years younger than me at least, and not wearing a long dress. 'Come back you creep.' I lose him in seconds, of course, in the labyrinth of lanes. The cobbles are slippery, and my flip-flops don't help, I have my hair in my eyes and my dress up round my knees. Rounding the corner, I cannon into two figures grappling for ownership of my bag and they separate like skittles. I grab a wayward arm to stop myself completely falling over as the other figure runs off.

'Whoa there! Are you OK?' The stranger steadies me and holds out my bag. 'This must be yours?'

I look past him to see where the other guy has gone, my heart pounding, but can't see very far down the shady passage.

'Oh gosh, thank you,' I gasp, taking the bag. 'Thank you so much.' I step back as he moves to pick up his jacket ... and the crash helmet that had clattered across the cobbles. What the hell? My brain racing to catch up. 'It's you!'

He grins sheepishly, 'You are one crazy lady; chasing after that guy like that.'

'I'm so sorry, are you OK? ... wait, are you following us?' Then it dawns on me how it must have looked earlier; I'd paid him too. This is so embarrassing. 'You're not really a taxi, are you?'

He shakes his head, 'But it was fun ... wasn't it?' His mouth twitches, and I catch his eye and then look away quickly.

He walks me back to the others, 'Are you ladies lost? Would you like a guide to show you around Tangier?' He offers me a card from his jacket pocket. It reads Tarik Tangier Tours.

'No honestly, thank you, we'll be fine now,' I slip his card into my purse, 'You've been very kind.'

'Well, you have my number if you change your mind. Please be careful.' He turns to me. Did he bow, even just slightly? And then he's gone, melting into the Medina, having saved me from another crisis.

Ignoring questioning looks from Marianne and Babs, we make off back towards the souk. I know they'll quiz me later. We find a small souvenir shop and I chuckle as Marianne focuses on forcing herself into a one-size-fits-all kaftan, determined to have at least one souvenir from the day. Stepping out of the door, our way is blocked by what can only be described as a giant, almost filling the entire space. He's wearing a blood-stained apron with a fat ewe draped, like an ermine collar, around his neck. He clutches all four sheep's hooves in one massive hand whilst waving us past with a meat cleaver in the other. His roar of laughter cuts the air and I stand petrified, my poor stomach contents doing that boiling rise to the back of my throat.

'Come on Jessie,' Barbara steers me away in the other direction, 'I think we could all do with a drink.' The butcher's laughter dies away only to be replaced by a frenzied bleating. Our eyes are drawn up to three little white faces with wobbling pink tongues frantically poking through the railings of a balcony. How did they get up there? I can sense their agitation and turn away just in time to avoid tripping over a steaming bucket of sheep's entrails. Hanging from a bracket directly above this, like a floral arrangement, is a dead sheep dripping red.

'Oh my God, I can't bear it,' I stagger back. My feet are like lead and my knees buckle under me. I begin to say I need to lie down, but my ears start buzzing, 'I feel ....,' my vision diminishes into a minute speck and then black ... and nothing.

I come to, hearing Babs' authoritative voice, 'Jessica, take it easy, pass me some water someone, quick.' My tongue tingles and my lips feel like they have pins and needles, I try to remember where I am.

'Here, I have some. Will she be OK?' Citrus and sandalwood restore my depleted senses like smelling salts. I open my eyes. Mr Tarik Tangier Tours. Oh God.

'What's happened?' he looks around at the others. 'I can't leave you ladies for five minutes.'

'We're not having a great day, I forgot about the festival.' Marianne's understatement is not lost on any of us. 'Poor Jessica here is vegan, it's all been a bit too much.' I discreetly tidy my hair by pulling it around to one side of my neck, and assume an elegant posture – as far as is possible sitting on cobbles.

'Ahh, yes, the sheep sacrifice.' He looks back down at me thoughtfully. 'Well, here in Morocco, they remember Abraham surrendering his son to God.' He continues, 'it's a tradition, perhaps you should have come for the jazz festival in June instead?' He gets a weak smile out of me and helps me back on my feet. 'You ladies could do with some lunch I think. Come, join me and my friends.'

I whimper. But the others don't need a second invitation; they're hot and bothered, hungry and thirsty. I have my emergency granola bars.

He leads us up several more flights of steps and the air becomes thick and sickening with the smell of burning bone and singed wool. We wind our way further, through a network of walkways, and gradually a smoky sweet aroma of barbequed meat drifts over courtyard gates and makes our tummies grumble, even mine. Eventually we reach a large restaurant where the whole of Tangier seems to be having lunch.

Tarik puts a hand on my arm, 'Don't worry Jessica, we'll find you something you can eat.'

* * *

I fidget, for the umpteenth time, with the dog-eared card. It has been weeks since our trip, and I'm getting itchy feet. Perhaps Tarik can recommend somewhere ... I'm ready for a new adventure.

On the third try I let the call go as far as to ring and, before I can change my mind, he picks up.

'Jessica!'

I'm thrilled at his note of happy surprise. 'You remember?'

'Of course, I remember you - my crazy lady.'

My courage grows as I outline the reason for my call.

'I can definitely recommend somewhere ... but how about I show you ... The Imilchil is on in September, in the Middle Atlas Mountains.'

'Is that another festival? I'm cringing already.'

'Why don't you come and see?'

Currant Tensions

Christine Hogg

'Brrring Brrrring.'

Rita sighed as the phone rang yet again. It was lovely of everyone to keep in touch, she really did appreciate it, but they didn't half pick their times. She looked at the phone display: her son, Kelvin.

She took a quick gulp of tea and a big bite of the toasted currant teacake that she'd just coated liberally with best butter. Rita chewed furiously, almost dislodging her dentures, cramming in as much as possible before she had to answer. She didn't dare not pick up, not after all that palaver with him ringing the neighbours last time, worrying everyone over nothing. She took another swift bite. Butter ran down her chin and she reached for a hankie.

The ringing stopped.

'Bugger.'

Rita wiped the butter off her chin and reached for the phone to call back, then paused and looked at her plate. Half a teacake was still sitting there, the surface shiny and yellow, melted butter dripping over the edges, plump black currants dotted around the perfectly golden toasted edges.

'Oh well, might as well be hung for a sheep as for a lamb.'

She sank back into her armchair and took slow, small bites, savouring the warm, slippery salty-sweetness. Stretching out her legs, Rita placed her feet into the shaft of sunlight streaming through the gap in the net curtains. Digging her bare toes into the deep pile carpet, she remembered the day Harold had chosen it. How she'd fussed about spending so much, thinking a cheaper nylon one would have done just as well.

'You were right, Harold,' she whispered to the empty room and closed her eyes, smiling.

'Brrring Brrring.'

Rita jolted upright and reached for the phone.

'Kelvin love, I was just going to call –'

'Where have you been?'

'I was just –'

'Why didn't you answer?'

'I was just in the middle of –'

Rita sank back in the chair and held the phone away from her ear as Kelvin's voice droned on. He meant well, but good heavens did he make mountains out of molehills. She took a deep breath and waited until finally there was a pause.

'Well love, no harm done,' she said cheerily.

'No harm?' Kelvin yelled.

Rita cringed. When had her gentle little toddler turned into this barking man?

'No harm? You could have been –'

'For heaven's sake,' Rita finally snapped. 'Yes, I could have been dead on the carpet. But I'm not.'

'What? ... I didn't mean –'

'I was eating a sodding currant teacake. Enjoying a bit of peace.'

'But I –'

'I've spent the whole morning on the phone. Have you put me on some kind of list? I've had calls from the council, calls from the village community group, even the vicar wanting to know if I need a food parcel.'

'Oh ... well... Yes, I ... I mean, I thought –'

His sudden hesitancy reminded Rita of the time she'd caught him red-handed, trying to steal sweets out of the kitchen cupboard when he was six.

Rita sighed. 'I'm sorry love, it's not you. I know you mean well, but I hate being at the top of a do-gooder's agenda. I'm staying in, following instructions, but there's only so much help I can take, however many well-wishers want to shop for me.'

There was silence from the other end of the phone line.

Rita bit her lip, then tried again. 'So ... How are you?'

'Fine,' said Kelvin.

'Mary?'

'She's fine.'

'The kids?'

'Fine. We are all completely fine.'

Rita rubbed her forehead and took a deep breath.

'Kelvin, love,' she said gently, picturing the six-year-old sulking in his shorts and hand-knitted jumper. 'I've said I'm sorry.'

Kelvin gave a non-committal grunt.

'Did you want anything in particular?' she asked.

Kelvin snorted. 'Not sure I dare say now.'

'Go on, love.'

'I'm at the supermarket. They've finally got toilet rolls back in stock. I know you said you had plenty, but I thought ...'

Rita pictured the mountain of toilet paper crammed under her bathroom sink. She'd always kept in front, just in case. Another pack of twelve had been dropped off by the neighbour yesterday, delighted they were back in at the village shop. She sighed.

'Thanks love,' she said. 'Very thoughtful.' She hadn't the heart to turn him down. Then she grinned. 'I tell you what you could do. Can you see if they've got any currant teacakes?'

Good Things Come To Those Who Wait

Susan O'Neal

'All good things come to those who wait.' Ellie had this dinned into her since she was very little. Be modest, don't make a fuss. Wait to be noticed. She waited to be asked to dance at the town disco. The handsome hunk she fancied was immediately commandeered by Loretta, all tousled blonde curls and sticky pouty lips. Ellie drank flat cider and waited. She was quite glad her dad turned up early to take her home.

At the next monthly disco, spotting Loretta again, in a very tight dress with her blonde curls topped with a huge red bow, she sighed. She was pretty much resigned to her own fate. She watched as the girl danced in the middle of the room by herself, eyes closed, swaying to the music blasting from the speakers. She noticed the good-looking boy was in the crowd hovering near Loretta. They were all waiting until she opened her eyes, hoping she would pick one of them. Ellie watched closely, trying to work out how Loretta did it. To her surprise, when Loretta did open those china-blue eyes, she looked right at Ellie and beckoned.

Ellie pushed off from the wall she had been leaning against and stepped on to the dance area.

'Wanna dance?' said Loretta.

'Yeah, I guess.'

It wasn't really dancing, what they were doing, they hardly moved their feet, flexing hips and shoulders in time to the beat. Ellie discovered she rather enjoyed being the centre of attention. Without looking, she knew all the boys were watching them.

'Living the dream,' she murmured.

Loretta leaned in close.

'The dream is free. The hustle takes a bit more effort,' she announced conspiratorially.

'What do you mean?' asked Ellie.

'I saw you at the last thing. You were waiting to be asked. You've got it the wrong way round. If you want something, it's okay praying for it, but in my experience you get even better results if you get up off your knees and hustle.'

She giggled as she watched Ellie digesting the advice.

'All these years-'

'Uh-huh. Let's not waste another moment.'